RESEARCH AND SOURCE GUIDE
FOR STUDENTS IN
SPEECH PATHOLOGY AND AUDIOLOGY

RESEARCH AND SOURCE GUIDE

FOR STUDENTS IN

SPEECH PATHOLOGY AND AUDIOLOGY

By

GORDON F. HOLLOWAY, Ph.D.

Chief, Audiology and Speech Pathology
Veterans Administration Center
Hot Springs, South Dakota

and

L. MICHAEL WEBSTER, Ph.D.

Director and Professor
School of Human Communication Disorders
Faculty of Health Professions
Dalhousi University
Halifax, Nova Scotia, Canada

DEO VERITATI INTELLIGENTIAE

WARREN H. GREEN, INC.

St. Louis, Missouri, U.S.A.

Published by

WARREN H. GREEN, INC.
8356 Olive Blvd
St. Louis, Missouri 63132, U.S.A.

Library of Congress Catalog Card No. 73-571
ISBN NO. 87527-154-5

Printed in the United States of America

PREFACE

The professions of Speech Pathology and Audiology are relatively new. Speech Pathology emerged as a professional entity in the 1920's when speech and hearing services were initiated in several public schools. Also at about the same time, three individuals (Sarah Stinchfield Hawk, Robert West and Lee Travis) received their doctorates. While their doctorates were received in other disciplines, the emphasis was on Speech Pathology. One of these pioneers, Lee Travis, developed the first program to offer specialized training in Speech Pathology during the early 1930's. During the same period, the American Speech Correction Association was formed.[1]

Audiology grew out of efforts by speech pathologists and otologists to rehabilitate the war deafened. Sometime during the early part of 1943 a rehabilitation program was established at Walter Reed General Hospital. The Otology Division, charged with administering the program soon recognized the magnitude of the problems associated with rehabilitating the hearing impaired. On November 1, 1943, the program was moved to Deshon General Hospital and established as a service separate from medical or surgical services. The program established at Deshon General Hospital included otologists, psychologists, speech pathologists and lipreading

[1]Students interested in further exploration of the history of Speech Pathology and Audiology are directed to Paden, E. P. *A History of the American Speech and Hearing Association,* 1938-1958. (Washington, D. C., ASHA, 1970)

instructors. The merger of interests of these professional groups in an effort to rehabilitate the hearing impaired resulted in the birth of a separate profession, audiology.

Speech Pathology and Audiology both are professions concerned with disordered communication and thus share common interests and problems when dealing with a communicatively impaired individual. It is appropriate that the two be joined together in a common professional association, the American Speech and Hearing Association, formerly the American Speech Correction Association.

Inasmuch as both professional areas are relatively young, there are yet many opportunities for valuable research contributions to be made. The purpose of this book is to provide the student with information which will allow him to pursue undergraduate research assignments or term papers with direction, thus providing a foundation for future research efforts. The book may also be useful to the graduate student whose baccalaureate education may have been deficient in these areas. The material has been arranged to: (1) provide a broad overview of research; (2) guide the student through the steps necessary to develop a research paper; (3) offer advice and suggestions for research proposals and projects, and (4) make him aware of the necessary and available sources.

ACKNOWLEDGEMENT

The cooperation of Mrs. Elaine Jackle Taylor and Mrs. Lynn C. Brewster in giving permission to publish their manuscripts, and the many hours of assistance provided by Ms. Joyce Kaufman, Ms. Betty Lindsey and Ms. Onamae Nelson in preparing the entire manuscript are most gratefully acknowledged.

G.F.H.
L.M.W.

CONTENTS

RESEARCH AND SOURCE GUIDE
FOR STUDENTS IN
SPEECH PATHOLOGY AND AUDIOLOGY

CHAPTER 1

AN INTRODUCTION TO RESEARCH IN SPEECH PATHOLOGY AND AUDIOLOGY

The present state of the art and science of Speech Pathology and Audiology is due largely to advancements made as the result of research. Centuries ago investigations demonstrated that surgery of the tongue did not relieve stuttering and that the deaf individual is in fact capable of reason. Research results constantly provide new evidence that alters therapy, suggests new diagnostic approaches, or indicates new rehabilitation designs. This is as it should be for the purpose of research is to improve our understanding and way of doing things by additions to and adaptations of present knowledge.

Research that focuses upon the nature of things is usually called natural science research; the behavioral sciences focus upon the behavior of people. Most research in the field of Speech Pathology and Audiology falls into the latter category. We also frequently make a distinction between pure and applied research. Pure research is undertaken for the sake of knowledge alone, without consideration of social values. Applied research is undertaken specifically to achieve some desired social goal. While we may differentiate between pure and applied research, the difference is often superficial, for while pure research findings have no immediate practical applications, they may later be the basis for important social developments.

There are three general types of research that need to be considered: historical, descriptive and experimental. The discussion that follows will provide a brief review of these types.

HISTORICAL RESEARCH

Historical research is considered the oldest form of research. Because of this, perhaps, it is often assumed that historical research should be the sole property of the historian. But surely, such an assumption is erroneous, for historical research may be applied not only to subject matter that is referred to as history, but also to establish the meaning and reliability of past facts in science, medicine, religion, and any other discipline. Historical research might also be called documentary research, since it consists of logically organizing evidence derived from documents and records. The careful analysis of records and logical arrangement of facts derived from them allows one to form conclusions which either establish facts previously unknown, or to develop generalizations with respect to past or present events, human motives, characteristics and thoughts.

What is to be gained from historical research? Why spend time studying documents? Most of us are curious about past events and this curiosity may provide justification enough. But beyond that, the method allows us to make generalizations from past events which may guide us. We study records of past and present to understand them, to learn something about their authors, and to make generalizations about them.

Documents that may be studied:

1. *Official records.* These include legislative, judicial, or executive documents prepared by federal, state or local governments, committee reports, vital statistics, etc.

2. *Personal records.* Personal papers, diaries, lecture notes, wills, deeds are not edited by their writers with any thought of publication, and so may reveal more detail than public records.

3. *Published materials.* Many publications such as newspapers, pamphlets, periodical articles, and texts convey valuable information.

Criticism of Documents

A researcher cannot assume that a record presents an authentic account of past events. He must examine each carefully to determine if the document is trustworthy. The researcher needs to demonstrate that the document he is dealing with is authentic; therefore, he needs to prove authorship, certify the date and place of origin and its textual accuracy. This process of determining the validity of a document is called *external criticism.* Pertinent questions which should be asked are: (1) Are the content, style and general tone of the document typical of the author's work? (2) Did the author write about events that he could have known? (3) Did the author exhibit ignorance of things that a man of his training should have known?

Once an external appraisal has been made one must turn to a critical analysis of the text itself. This process, *internal criticism,* should lead to an understanding of the meaning of the document. The criticism must center around questions directed to the text. (1) Are the statements by the author credible? (2) How soon after the particular event was the text written? (3) Was the truth distorted in order to achieve literary style?

Historical Research in Speech Pathology and Audiology

The historical research in Speech Pathology and Audiology has generally been of two types; the development of the profession and trends studies. The trends studies have considered trends in therapeutic approaches, instrumentation, training practices, and diagnostic procedures. The information gained from such studies helps place the profession in proper perspective, and provides professional direction. A question one must periodically ask relative to professional activity is: Which new directions are being considered? The information gained from studies that review past and present practices and emerging changes can provide answers.

The student can learn much about the profession of Speech Pathology and Audiology by reviewing available historical research. Additionally, a search of documents, diaries, journals and so forth, can prove to be a rewarding experience and provide interesting and perhaps, valuable information relative to the profession.

Selected Bibliography

The following entries are but examples of historical research in speech pathology and audiology as well as material which may be of value if the student wishes to pursue this type of research as a project.

Bluemel, C.S.: Concepts of Stammering: A Century in Review. *Journal of Speech and Hearing Disorders,* XXV (February, 1960), 24-32.

Morris, Delyte, *et al.*: Speech, Voice, and Hearing Disorders Bibliography for the years 1933-1936. *Journal of Speech Disorders,* I (February, 1937), 27-34.

Paden, E.: *A History of the American Speech and Hearing Association, 1938-1958.* Washington, D. C.: ASHA, 1970.

Schoolfield, Lucille: The Development of Speech Correction in America in the Nineteenth Century. *Quarterly Journal of Speech,* XXIV (February, 1938), 101-116.

Sies, L. and Schwimmer, A.: Samuel D. Robbins: Autobiographical Reminiscences. *ASHA,* XIV (June, 1972), 345-348.

Strother, Charles: Trends in Speech Pathology. *Quarterly Journal of Speech,* XXIX (February, 1943), 76-80.

DESCRIPTIVE RESEARCH

The purpose of descriptive research is to assess the present status of phenomena. This type of research leads to answers to questions such as: What is the nature of prevailing attitudes and practices? Where are we? Where should we be? While descriptive research seeks answers to these questions, it is not confined to routine fact finding. Researchers are interested also in identifying relationships (among and between variables) and making predictions based upon their findings.

There are three general types of research studies employing the descriptive method in Speech Pathology and Audiology; developmental, survey, and case studies.

Developmental Studies

Developmental studies are concerned with the existing status of phenomena and with changes that take place as a function of time. Investigators engaged in developmental studies describe variables in the course of their development over a period of months or years.

Much of the information available to us today relative to the normal acquisition of speech and language has been the result of developmental studies.

Survey Studies

This method of research attempts to describe a condition or to learn the status of a situation. The objective of the researcher may be not only to determine status but also to determine the adequacy of status by comparing it with established standards. Common survey studies included educational surveys, public opinion surveys and community surveys.

One of the most effective means of obtaining data for a survey study is the personal interview. Interviewing techniques are difficult and must be performed in a more exacting manner than the inexperienced might suspect. One should keep the following points in mind when preparing for an interview: (1) develop a detailed interview plan; (2) gain the confidence of the respondent, and (3) be prepared to accurately record the information provided.

Another effective means of acquiring data is the questionnaire. This method may offer some advantages over the interview. The questionnaire can be distributed over a large geographical area, thus saving the time and money that would be required if one were to travel for interviews. The questionnaire consists of a series of written questions. However, because the interviewer is not available to clarify questions, the questions must be carefully formulated.

Then too, mailing questionnaires does not guarantee a response. Inasmuch as the purpose of the questionnaire is to obtain data, it must be planned carefully in order to gain maximum return from the respondents. Some basic rules for preparing the questionnaire follow:

(1) Clearly explain the purpose of the study.

(2) Give clear, complete directions.

(3) Keep the questionnaire as brief as possible.

(4) State the questions in clear and simple language.

(5) Arrange the items in a logical sequence.

Case Studies

Researchers may wish to go beyond the process of collecting facts to obtain an accurate assessment of an existing situation; they may trace inter-relationships between facts in an effort to gain deeper insight into phenomena, and it is the case study that allows him to obtain the detailed information necessary to establish these inter-relationships.

In essence, the case study amounts to a thorough examination of the life and behavior of an individual or single social unit. The researcher compiles all the available data regarding the life history of the subject, the inter-relations that have affected it, and the evolving picture of its present status.

While case studies often produce information useful to research, they do have limitations. For example, the student should be aware that information on one subject or patient cannot be extrapolated to cover the entire population of people similarly classified. The detailed nature of the case study may provide insights that may help formulate a hypothesis, or suggest factors to be looked for in other cases. The case study is commonly identified with therapy in the speech and hearing clinic. Part of the evaluation process in preparing a therapeutic program for a client consists of a careful interview for a history of the problem, family background examination of medical reports, testing, etc.

Selected Bibliography

The studies cited here for each type of

descriptive research serve as examples to the student. While the examples for the most part are random selections, those representing development research are considered classics.

Developmental Studies

Eisenberg, Rita, Griffin, E., and David Coursins: Auditory Behavior in the Human Neonate: A Preliminary Report. *Journal of Speech and Hearing Research,* VII (May, 1964), 245-269.

Griffiths, R.: *The Abilities of Babies.* New York, McGraw-Hill, 1954.

Irwin, Orvis: Phonetical Description of Speech Development in Children, in, L. Kaine (Ed.) *Manual of Phonetics.* Amsterdam, North Holland, 1957.

Poole, Irene: Genetic Development of Articulation of Consonant Sounds in Speech. *Elementary English Review,* XI (June, 1934), 159-161.

Templin, Mildren: *Certain Language Skills in Children.* Minneapolis, University of Minnesota, 1957.

Survey Studies

Anderson, John: Status of College and University Programs of Practicum in the Schools. *ASHA,* XV (January, 1973), 60-63.

Curlee, Richard: Status of Educational Training Programs in Speech Pathology and Audiology - 1971-1972. *ASHA,* XIV (September, 1972), 551-555.

Martin, Frederick and Carolyn Pennington: ASHA Audiologists: Professional Background Information. *ASHA,* XIV (May, 1972), 255-257.

Case Studies

Kolmin, Ira and Shimizu Hiroshi: Recovery from Aphasia as Monitored by AER Audiometry. *Journal of Speech and Hearing Disorders,* XXXVII (August, 1972), 414-420.

LaPointe, Leonard and Gerald Carlton: Visual-Spatial Neglect Subsequent to Brain-Injury. *Journal of Speech and Hearing Disorders,* XXXIV (February, 1969), 82-86.

Quinn, Galen and Raymond Massensill, Jr.: The Use of a Bilateral Speech Appliance in Conjunction with a Pharyngeal Flap: Two Case Reports. *Journal of Speech and Hearing Disorders*, XXXVI (August, 1971), 422-424.

Strandberg, Twila, Jerry Griffith and Mack Hollowell: A Case Study of Psychogenic Hoarseness. *Journal of Speech and Hearing Disorders,* XXXVI (1971), 281-286.

EXPERIMENTAL RESEARCH

The term experiment is frequently used in conversation and by children as well as adults. It may conjure very different mental images but the basic concept is essentially the same. The child may visualize the mad scientist with bubbling liquids and flashing lights about to perform some strange "experiment." The student may "experiment" by altering a certain phase of his study habits to note the effect it may have upon his grades. The speech pathologist may compare two therapy techniques to determine the rate of speech improvement brought about by each. In each case, controlled action, or manipulation is implied. Werkmeister has pointed out that experimentation ". . . consists of the deliberate and controlled modification of the conditions determining an event, and in the observation and interpretation of the ensuing changes in the event itself."[1] Careful reading of the statement suggests that there are three basic concepts in experimental research: ". . .deliberate and controlled (control) modification of the conditions (variable) determining an event (causation). . ."

Causation

The concept of causation expresses a one-to-one relationship. When any two phenomena are associated, one taking place before the other, and one is an indispensable and variable antecedent of the other, the first is the cause of the second.

A phenomena called delayed auditory feedback (DAF) illustrates the concept of causation nicely. When the average speaker listens to his own speech through earphones and the speech fed to his ear is delayed by an electronic apparatus his ongoing speech becomes disorganized. The delay is the "indispensible and invariable antecedent" of the disrupted speech;

---

[1]Werkmeister, W. *An Introduction to Critical Thinking.* (Lincoln: Johnson Publishing Company, 1948, 618-619)

the first (delay in feedback) is the cause of the second (disrupted speech).

Variable

The process of experimentation requires precision; it is not a blind trial-and-error procedure. We made the point when discussing causation that when only two phenomena are associated, one taking place before the other, and one of them an "indispensable and invariable antecedent" of the other, the first is the cause of the second. The phenomenon which occurs first is the *independent variable* and serves to determine the outcome of the event following, the *dependent variable.* This relationship may be more clearly recognized below:

Independent variable		Dependent variable
condition x	*is related*	*condition y*

The experimenter, wishing to determine the effects of a particular variable upon another manipulates the independent variable and notes the resultant change in the dependent variable.

We may examine such manipulation in light of the previous phenomenon discussed, DAF. It has been established that the most effective speech delay is .2 second. How was this value determined? Through experimentation. The experimenter manipulated the independent variable (delay time) while observing the fluency characteristics of the speaker. The greatest speech disruption occurred at .2 second. This delay time, the antecedent event, caused the second, i.e., the response is dependent upon the antecedent event.

Control

At this point, the reader may feel that experimental investigation is relatively simple; that is not so. The experimenter does not merely manipulate one variable to see what happens to another; he uses controlled observations. The control of the independent variable is essential to experimental research, for only careful control of the independent variable will allow the experimenter to conclude that manipulation of this variable and not some extraneous variable produced the observed results of the dependent variable. In other words, while manipulating the individual variable, all other pertinent variables must remain constant.

Careful control offers several important consequences: (1) the experiment can be repeated; (2) the event can be made to occur when the experimenter wishes them allowing him to be prepared to observe, and (3) the results can be systematically recorded.[2]

There is a myriad of experimental reports available ranging from simple and straightforward investigations of one concise area to lengthy investigations. The following specific references provide examples of experimental studies.

Selected Bibliography

Johnson, Wendell: *Stuttering in Children and Adults.* Minneapolis: University of Minnesota Press, 1955.

[2]For a more elaborate treatment of experimental design and the essentials of control, etc., the reader is encouraged to seek texts such as: Kerlinger, F.N.: *Foundation of Behavioral Research.* (New York: Holt, Rhinehart and Winston, 1964).

Ventry, Ira, Joseph Chaiklin and Richard Dixon: *Hearing Measurement: A Book of Readings.* (New York: Appleton-Centry-Crofts, 1971).

THE RESEARCH PROJECT - GENERAL

The purpose of a research project at the beginning level is twofold. First it provides the opportunity for the student to become acquainted with many journals which are germane to the profession of Speech Pathology and Audiology. Second, it forces the student to read widely in a subject area, integrate the broad information, and combine it into a single logical unit.

The research project *should* represent an interesting challenge to the student; most often it represents frustration. The authors feel the frustration is due to two factors; procrastination by the student and/or too little information about the procedures involved in carrying out a research project. The order is not intended to suggest that the authors consider student procrastination the most frequent contributor to frustration associated with research projects. Their own experiences, however, make it highly suspect.

The obvious advice to the student is *plan your project carefully* so you do not find yourself out of time and panic stricken. When this occurs *you* are the loser because you have failed to experience the excitement of discovery, of learning new facts and of gaining new professional insights.

The steps necessary to conduct a research project are not difficult. First, one must *make a broad survey* of the literature. Questions which might be asked are: What topics interest me? What source material is available? Is instrumentation required? Is it available? Do I have the background necessary to understand the topic of interest?

After considering these questions one needs then to *narrow the topic* in order to keep it within reasonable limits. The undergraduate research project is usually quite limited in scope. One could not, for example, in a reasonable time complete a research project that covered "Audiology." One could, however, develop a concise project that discussed "Public School Hearing Screening."

Once the research project has been planned and the information gathered, the *paper has to be written.* This step is critical. The student who organizes his research project skillfully and gathers his information accurately, but fails to communicate his findings, has wasted his efforts. Organization of the written report is vital to the research project for the report clearly defines how the researcher designed the project, how he gathered the information, and the results of his efforts.

CHAPTER II

THE RESEARCH PAPER

Selecting a topic and locating sources

Throughout their education, majors in speech pathology and audiology are very often required to write a research paper as a partial requirement for many of their courses. The paper may fall into any of the categories already mentioned (historical, descriptive or experimental). This section will offer lists of selected references which should aid the student in selecting a topic and direct him to sources of information specifically directed at that topic. Generally speaking, most papers require either a broad presentation, such as is suggested by a title like, "Speech Pathology—the Scope of the Profession," or, they require an elaboration of a rather specific topic, as is suggested by "Pure Tone Air-Conduction Testing." The former requires a list of survey sources whereas the latter requires a list of highly specific sources. Following is a selected list of annotated survey sources for both speech pathology and audiology. Next a list of references (non-annotated) will be offered which is designed to direct the student to specific interest areas in both speech pathology and audiology. It is not intended that any of these lists be conceived of as either comprehensive or exhaustive. They are designed to help the student get going. He is encouraged to use the bibliographies and lists of references to broaden his source of information. In another section of this book we will provide ways and means of locating other informational sources.

SURVEY SOURCES—SPEECH PATHOLOGY

Travis, Lee, Ed.: *The Handbook of Speech Pathology and Audiology.* Appleton-Centry-Crofts, 1971.

This book is the "classic" survey work of the profession and has been recently significantly updated. Chapters are now quite sophisticated, and the new student might benefit most for survey papers by reviewing the table of contents and the chapter on terminology. Older editions should not be ignored, as they allow for the tracing of growth in the profession.

Van Riper, Charles: *Speech Correction: Principles and Methods* (2nd ed.). Princeton: Prentice Hall, Incorporated, 1972.

A standard undergraduate survey text which is periodically and significantly updated. The student should not be misled by the title, inasmuch as the book is almost more informative about pathology than it is about principles and methods for correction.

Johnson, Wendell, *et al.: Speech Handicapped*

School Children (revised edition). Princeton: Harper and Brothers, 1956.

Another standard undergraduate survey text. Although occasionally revised, its contents remains relatively static. Much of the information is quite dated, but still useful in giving a general feeling of the scope of the profession. The chapter on stuttering is a classic in the field and probably the most comprehensive statement in the diagnosogenic or semantogenic theory of stuttering.

West, Robert, *et al.: The Rehabilitation of Speech.* New York: Harper and Brothers, 1947.

A truly classic text which was very comprehensive in its time. West's attempts to influence the nomenclature of the field along medical lines is clearly revealed in this book. As with Van Riper's book, the title is deceiving, inasmuch as the actual information about therapeutic techniques is relatively scant. Again, the scope of our interests becomes apparent by studying this book's contents, but the vast majority of the content is seriously dated.

Gray, Giles and Claude Wise: *The Basis of Speech.* New York: Harper and Rowe, 1959.

Not a book on pathologies of speech nor on rehabilitative techniques; rather a book based on the premise that the more one understands the nature and function of normal speech the better he is prepared to understand the processes of improving abnormal speech. Periodically (but not frequently enough), the books is updated and is an excellent resource for the undergraduate student.

Perkins, William: *Speech Pathology:* An Applied Behavioral Science. Baltimore: Mosley Company, 1971.

A more recent attempt to reveal the scope of speech pathology between the covers of one book. This book has been well received by reviewers and is likely to become a classic in the field. A large body of updated information is presented within a framework which is essentially a plea to the field to become more systematic and objective in its approach to studying and treating speech pathologies.

Denes, Peter and Elliott Pinson: *The Speech Chain.* Chicago: Bell Telephone Laboratories, 1963.

Although intended primarily to be an introductory book to the topic of speech science, this book serves well to delineate the areas of interest to those in speech pathology and audiology.

SURVEY SOURCES—AUDIOLOGY

Davis Hallowell and Richard Silverman, eds.: *Hearing and Deafness* (3rd ed.). New York: Rhinehart and Winston Incorporated, 1970.

This book provides an overview of the history

of audiology, fundamentals of physics and psychoacoustics, anatomy and physiology of the ear, ear pathologies and their medical and surgical treatment, aural rehabilitation procedures, psychology of hearing impairment, and vocational guidance for the hard of hearing. While some parts of the text may be difficult for undergraduate students, the major portion presents easy reading.

Newby, Hayes: *Audiology* (2nd ed.). New York: Appleton-Centry-Crofts, 1964.

The author presents a general overview of audiology and provides detailed procedures for performing various audiometric tests. The text is designed for beginning students in audiology and therefore presents easy reading.

Katz, Jack, ed.: *Handbook of Clinical Audiology.* Baltimore: Williams and Wilkins Company, 1972.

The *Handbook* presents a broad view of all aspects of clinical audiology including clinical testing, hearing aids, case history techniques and aural rehabilitation. The book is aimed primarily at graduate level students and researchers, but many chapters are not beyond the level of advanced undergraduate students.

O'Neill, John and Herbert Oyer: *Applied Audiometry.* New York: Dodd, Mead and Company, Incorporated, 1970.

Material is presented which is specific to audiometry, that is, audiometric testing procedures. The level of presentation is suitable for undergraduate students.

Sataloff, Joseph: *Hearing Loss.* New York: J.B. Lippincott Company, 1966.

The text is slanted toward providing information relative to audiometric testing for physicians and includes discussions of testing procedures and interpretations of audiometric results. The level of presentation is suitable for undergraduate students.

SPECIFIC SOURCES

The sources below are listed in chronological order so the student may pursue the historical development of speech pathology and audiology trends in testing procedures, as well as gaining detailed information about specific aspects of speech pathology and audiology. We reiterate that these lists are not intended to be exhaustive or comprehensive. For example, it will be noted that topics like cerebral palsy, mental retardation, etc., are not included.

Speech Pathology

Voice

1937

Jackson, D. and D. L. Jackson: *The Larynx and Its Diseases.* Philadelphia: Saunders.

1940

Curry, R.: *The Mechanism of the Human Voice.* New York: Longmans Greene and Company, Incorporated.

1942

Anderson, V.: *Training the Speaking Voice.* New York: Oxford.

Judson, L. and A. Weaver: *Voice Science.* New York: Appleton-Century Crofts.

1953

Brodnitz, F.: *Keep Your Voice Healthy.* New York: Harper.

1954

Moses, P.: *The Voice of Neurosis.* New York: Grune and Stratton.

1956

Curtis, J.: Disorders of Voice, in *Speech Handicapped School Children.* Ed. by W. Johnson, *et al.,* New York: Harper and Brothers.

1957

Hahn, E., *et al.: Basic Voice Training for Speech.* New York: McGraw Hill.

1958

Akin, J.: *And So We Speak: Voice and Articulation.* Englewood Cliffs: Prentice-Hall.

Eiseson, J. *The Improvement of Voice and Diction.* New York: MacMillan.

1959

McClosky, D.: *Your Voice at Its Best.* Boston: Little Brown, & Company.

1960

Fairbanks, G.: *Voice and Articulation Drillbook,* 2nd ed. New York: Harper and Brothers.

1962

Hanley, T., and W. Thurman: *Developing Vocal Skills.* New York: Holt, Rinehart and Winston.

Levin, N., ed.: *Voice and Speech Disorders: Medical Aspects.* Springfield: Charles C Thomas.

1964

Greene, M.: *The Voice and Its Disorders,* 2nd ed. London: Jittman.

Murphy, A.: *Functional Voice Disorders.* Englewood Cliffs: Prentice-Hall.

Myerson, V.: *The Human Larynx.* Springfield: Charles C Thomas.

1965

American Academy of Opthamology and Otolaryngology: *Vocal Rehabilitation.* Rochester, Minn.: American Academy of Opthamology and Otolaryngology.

Luchsinger, R., and G. Arnold: *Voice-Speech-Language Clinical Communicology: Its Physiology and Pathology.* Belmont: Wadsworth.

1968

Procter, D.: The Physiologic Basis of Voice Training, in *Sound Production in Man.* M. Krauss, ed., New York: York Academy of Sciences.

1971

Boone, D.: *The Voice and Voice Therapy.* Englewood Cliffs: Prentice-Hall.

Brackett, I.: Parameters of Voice Quality, in, *Handbook of Speech Pathology and Audiology.* L. Travis, ed., New York: Appleton-Century-Crofts.

Cooper, M.: Modern Techniques of Vocal Rehabilitation for Functional and Organic Dysphonias, in *Handbook of Speech Pathology and Audiology.* L. Travis, ed., New York: Appleton-Century-Crofts.

Michel, J., and R. Wendahl: Correlates of Voice Production, in, *Handbook of Speech Pathology and Audiology.* L. Travis, ed., New York: Appleton-Century-Crofts.

Moore, G.: Voice Disorders Organically Based in *Handbook of Speech Pathology and Audiology.* L. Travis, ed., New York Appleton-Century-Crofts.

Perkins, W.: Vocal Function: A Behavioral Analysis, in *Handbook of Speech Pathology and Audiology.* L. Travis, ed., New York: Appleton-Century Crofts.

1972

Wilson, D.: *Voice Problems of Children.* Baltimore: Wilkins and Wilkins.

1974

Moncur, J., and I. Brackett: *Modifying Vocal Behavior.* New York: Harper & Row.

Stuttering

1928

Fletcher, J.: *The Problem of Stuttering: A Diagnosis and a Plan of Treatment.* New York: Longmans.

1929

Appelt, A.: *Stammering and Its Permanent Cure.* London: Methuen.

1930

Fogerty, E.: *Stammering.* New York: Dutton.

1932

Boome, E., and M. Richardson: *The Nature and Treatment of Stammering.* New York: E. P. Dutton and Company.

1935

Bluemel, C.: *Stammering and Allied Disorders.* New York: MacMillan.

1937

Wedberg, C.: *The Stutterer Speaks.* Magnolia: Expression Company.

1940

Gifford, M.: *How to Overcome Stammering.* Englewood Cliffs: Prentice-Hall.

1941

Kingdon-Ward, E.: *Stammering,* London: Hamilton.

1943

Hahn, E.: *Stuttering, 1943: Significant Theories and Therapies.* Palo Alto: Stanford.

1950

Wilton, G.: *How to Overcome Stuttering.* New York: Harper and Brothers.

1954

Barbara, D.: *Stuttering: A Psychodynamic Approach to Its Understanding and Treatment.* New York: Julian Press.

1955

Johnson, W., ed.: *Stuttering in Children and Adults.* Minneapolis: University of Minnesota Press.

1957

Brook, F.: *Stammering and Its Treatment.* London: Pitman Publishing Company.

1958

Diehl, C.: *A Compendium of Research and Theory on Stuttering.* Springfield: Charles C Thomas.

1959

Johnson, W.: *The Onset of Stuttering.* Minneapolis: University of Minnesota Press.

1960

Murphy, A., and R. Fitzsimmons: *Stuttering and Personality Dynamics: Play Therapy, Projective Therapy and Counseling.* New York: Ronald.

1964

Andrews, G., and M. Harris: *The Syndrome of Stuttering.* London: Heineman.

Luper, H., and R. Mulder: *Stuttering Therapy for Children.* Englewood Cliffs: Prentice-Hall.

Robinson, F.: *An Introduction to Stuttering.* Englewood Cliffs: Prentice-Hall.

1966

Adler, S.: *A Clinician's Guide to Stuttering.* Springfield: Charles C Thomas.

Freund, H.: *Psychopathology and the Problems of Stuttering.* Springfield: Charles C Thomas.

1967

Brutten, E., and E. Shoemaker: *The Modification of Stuttering.* Englewood Cliffs: Prentice-Hall.

1968

Gregory, H., ed.: *Learning Theory and Stuttering Therapy.* Evanston: Northwestern University Press.

1969

Gray, B., and G. England: *Stuttering and the Conditioning Therapies.* Monterey: The Monterey Institute for Speech and Hearing.

1971

Travis, L., ed.: *Handbook of Speech Pathology and Audiology,* 2nd ed. New York: Appleton-Century-Crofts.

Van Riper, C.: Symptomatic Therapy for Stuttering, in, *Handbook for Speech Pathology and Audiology,* 2nd ed. L. Travis, ed., New York: Appleton-Century-Crofts.

Van Riper, C.: *The Nature of Stuttering.* Englewood Cliffs: Prentice-Hall.

Williams, D.: Stuttering Therapy for Children, in, *Handbook of Speech Pathology and Audiology,* 2nd ed. L. Travis, ed., New York: Appleton-Centry-Crofts.

1973

VanRiper, C.: *The Treatment of Stuttering.* New York: Prentice-Hall.

The non-copyrighted booklets which follow were published under a variety of dates. The booklets provide excellent information about stuttering and should be familiar to all speech pathology students. They will prove to be very beneficial in preparation of reports.

Speech Foundation of America: *Stuttering and*

Its Treatment. Memphis: Speech Foundation of America, 1961.
Speech Foundation of America: *Stuttering, Its Prevention.* Memphis: Speech Foundation of America, 1962.
Speech Foundation of America: *Stuttering Words.* Memphis: Speech Foundation of America, 1963.
Speech Foundation of America: *Treatment of the Stutterer in the School.* Memphis: Speech Foundation of America, 1964.
Speech Foundation of America: *Stuttering: Training the Therapist.* Memphis: Speech Foundation of America, 1966.
Speech Foundation of America: *Stuttering: Success and Failures in Therapy.* Memphis: Speech Foundation of America, 1968.

Aphasia

1931

Taylor, G., ed.: *Selected Writings of John Hughlings Jackson.* London: Hodder and Stoughton.

1932

Goldstein, K.: *After Effects of Brain Injuries in War.* New York: Grune and Stratton.

1935

Weisenburg, T., and L. McBride: *Aphasia.* New York: Commonwealth Fund.

1941

Neilson, J.: *A Textbook of Clinical Neurology.* New York: Paul Hoeber.

1947

Granich, L.: *Aphasia: A Guide to Retraining.* New York: Grune and Stratton.

Neilson, J.: *Agnosia, Apraxia, Aphasia,* 2nd ed. New York: Paul Hoeber.

Strauss, A., and L. Lehtinen: *Psychopathology and Education of the Brain-Injured Child.* Vol. I., New York: Grune and Stratton.

1948

Goldstein, K.: *Language and Language Disturbances.* New York: Grune and Stratton.

1949

Hebb, D.: *The Organization of Behavior.* New York: John Wiley and Sons.

1951

Wepman, J.: *Recovery from Aphasia.* New York: Ronald.

1954

McCarthy, D.: Language Development in Children, in, *Manual of Child Psychology.* L. Carmichael, ed., New York: John Wiley and Sons.

Myklebust, H.: *Auditory Disorders in Children: A Manual for Differential Diagnosis.* New York: Grune and Stratton.

1955

Allport, F.: *Theories of Perception and a Concept of Structure.* New York: John Wiley and Sons.

1958

Neff, W., and L. Diamond: The Neural Basis of Auditory Discrimination, in, *Biological and Biochemical Bases of Behavior.* H. Harlow and C. Woolsey, eds., Madison: University of Wisconsin Press.

1959

Penfield, W., and L. Roberts: *Speech and Brain Mechanisms.* Princeton: Princeton.

Taylor, M., and M. Marks: *Aphasia Rehabilitation and Therapy Kit.* New York: Saxon.

1961

Cruickshank, W.: *A Training Method for Hyperactive Children.* Syracuse: Syracuse University Press.

Russel, W., and M. Espir: *Traumatic Aphasia.* London: Oxford University Press.

Schuell, H.: The Nature of Language Deficit in Aphasia, in, *Psycholinguistics.* S. Saporta, ed., New York: Holt, Rinehart, and Winston.

1963

Luria, A.: *Restoration of Function after Brain Injury.* New York: MacMillan.

McGinnis, M.: *Aphasic Children.* New York: Volta Bureau.

Magoun, H.: *The Waking Brain,* 2nd ed. Springfield: Charles C Thomas.

1964

Rioch, D., and E. Weinstein, eds.: *Disorders of Communication.* Baltimore: Williams and Wilkins.

Schuell, H., J. Jenkins and E. Jimenez-Pabon: *Aphasia in Adults.* New York: Harper and Row.

Weisenberg, T., and R. McBride: *Aphasia: A Clinical and Psychological Study.* New York: Hafner.

1965

Jones, L., and J. Wepman: Language: A Perspective from the Study of Aphasia, in, *Directions in Psycholinguistics.* S. Rosenberg, ed., New York: MacMillan.

Myklebust, H.: *Development and Disorders of Written Language.* Vol. I., New York: Grune and Stratton.

1967

Johnson, D., and H. Myklebust: *Learning Disabilities: Educational Principles and Practices.* New York: Grune and Stratton.

Milliken, C., and F.·Darley: *Brain Mechanisms Underlying Speech and Language.* New York: Grune and Stratton.

1968

Geschwind, N.: Neurological Foundations of Language, in, *Progress in Learning Disabilities.* Vol. I., H. Myklebust, ed., New York: Grune and Stratton.

McGrady, H.: Language Pathology and Learning Disabilities, in, *Progress in Learning Disabilities.* Vol. I., H. Myklebust, Ed., New York: Grune and Stratton.

1972

Sarno, M.: *Aphasia: Selected Readings.* New York: Appleton-Century-Crofts.

1975

Brookshire, R.: *An Introduction to Aphasia.* Minneapolis: BRK Publications.

Articulation

1923

Scripture, E.: *Stuttering, Lisping and Correction of the Speech of the Deaf* New York: MacMillan.

1931

Travis, L.: *Speech Pathology.* New York: Appleton-Century-Crofts.

1935

Set, G., and D. Guthrie: *Speech in Childhood.* London: Oxford University Press.

1936

Cotrel, E., and E. Halted: *Class Lessons for Improving Speech.* Boston: Expression Company.

Koepp-Baker, H.: *A Handbook of Clinical Speech.* Ann Arbor: Edwards Brothers.

1937

Nemoy, E., and S. Davis: *The Correction of Defective Consonant Sounds.* Boston: Expression Company.

1939

Mulgrave, C.: *Speech for the Classroom Teacher.* Englewood Cliffs: Prentice-Hall.

1940

McCullough, G.: *Speech Improvement Work and Practice Book.* Boston: Expression Company.

1942

Berry, M., and J. Eisenson: *The Defective in Speech.* New York: Appleton-Century-Crofts.

1943

Backus, O.: *Speech in Education.* New York: Longmans.

1947

Van Riper, C.: *Speech Correction Principles and Methods,* 2nd ed. Englewood Cliffs: Prentice-Hall.

West, R., L. Kennedy, and A. Carr: *The Rehabilitation of Speech.* New York: Harper.

1948

Ainsworth, S.: *Speech Correction Methods.* Englewood Cliffs: Prentice-Hall.

1950

Johnson, W.: *Speech Problems of Children.* New York: Grune and Stratton.

1951

Backus, O., and J. Beasley: *Speech Therapy with Children.* Boston: Houghton Mifflin.

Lewis, M.: *Infant Speech, A Study of the Beginnings of Language.* New York: Humanities Press.

Schoolfield, L.: *Better Speech and Better Reading.* Boston: Expression Company.

Stetson, R.: *Motor Phonetics: A Study of Speech Movements in Action.* Amersterdam: North Holland Publishing Company.

1952

Raubicheck, L.: *Speech Improvement.* Englewood Cliffs: Prentice-Hall.

1953

Anderson, V.: *Improving the Child's Speech.* New York: Oxford.

Irwin, R.: *Speech and Hearing Therapy.* Englewood Cliffs: Prentice-Hall.

1954

Nemoy, E.: *Speech Correction Through Story-Telling Units.* Boston: Expression Company.

1955

Zedler, E.: *Listening for Speech Sounds.* Garden City, New York: Doubleday.

1956

Johnson, W., S. Brown, J. Curtis, C. Edney, and J. Keaster: *Speech Handicapped School Children.* New York: Harper

1957

Powers, M.: Functional Disorders of Articulation—Symptomology and Etiology, in *Handbook of Speech Pathology.* L. Travis, ed., New York: Appleton-Century-Crofts.

1958

Van Riper, C. and J. Irwin: *Voice and Articulation.* Englewood Cliffs: Prentice-Hall.

Templin, M.: *Certain Language Skills in Children.* Minneapolis: University of Minnesota Press.

1963

Van Riper, C.:*Speech Correction Principles and Methods,* 4th ed. Englewood Cliffs: Prentice-Hall.

Johnson, W., F. Darley, and D. Spriestersbach: *Diagnostic Methods in Speech Pathology.* New York and Evanston: Harper and Row.

1964

McDonald, E.: *Articulation Testing and Treatment: A Sensory Motor Approach.* Pittsburgh: Stanwix House.

1966

Templin, M.: The Study of Articulation and

Language Development During the Early School Years, in, *The Genesis of Language.* G. Miller and F. Smith, eds., Cambridge: Michigan Institute of Technology Press.

Milisen, R.: Articulatory Problems, in, *Speech Pathology.* R. Reiber and R. Brubaker, eds., Amsterdam: North-Holland Publishing Company.

1967

Bernstein, N.: *The Coordination and Regulation of Movements.* Long Island City: Permagon Press, Incorporated.

Bloomer, H.: Oral Manifestations of Dydiadokokinesis with Oral Asteriognosia, in, *Symposium on Oral Sensation and Perception,* J. Bosma, ed., Springfield: Charles C Thomas.

1968

Carrell, J.: *Disorders of Articulation.* Englewood Cliffs: Prentice-Hall.

West, R., and M. Ansberry: *The Rehabilitation of Speech.* New York: Harper and Row.

1969

Winitz, H.: *Articulatory Acquisition and Behavior.* New York: Appleton-Century-Crofts.

1971

Perkins, W.: *Speech Pathology, An Applied Behavioral Science.* Saint Louis: C. V. Mosby Company.

Travis, L.: *Handbook of Speech Pathology and Audiology.* New York: Appleton-Century-Crofts.

1973

Minifie, F., J. Hixon, and F. Williams: *Normal Aspects of Speech, Hearing and Language.* Englewood Cliffs: Prentice Hall.

1974

Emerick, L. and J. Hatten: *Diagnosis and Evaluation in Speech Pathology.* Englewood Cliffs: Prentice Hall.

Dickson, S. ed.: *Communication Disorders: Remedial Principles and Practices.* Chicago: Scott-Forsman and Co.

1975

Darley, F. A., Aaronson, R. and Brown.: *Motor Speech Disorders.* Toronto: W. B. Saunders.

1976

Mysak, E.: *Pathologies of Speech Systems.* Baltimore: Wilkins and Wilkins.

Language

1953

Carrol, J.: *The Study of Language.* Cambridge: Harvard.

1957

Skinner, B.: *Verbal Behavior.* New York: Appleton-Century-Crofts.

Templin, M.: *Certain Language Skills in Children.* Minneapolis: University of Minnesota Press.

Whatmough, J.: *Language: A Modern Synthesis.* New York: Mentor Books.

1959

Penfield, W., and L. Roberts: *Speech and Brain Mechanisms.* Princeton: Princeton University Press.

1960

Berko, J., and R. Brown: Psycholinguistic Research Methods, in, *Handbook of Research Methods in Child Development.* P. Mussen, ed., New York: Wiley.

Mowrer, O.: *Learning Theory and the Symbolic Processes.* New York: Wiley.

1961

Gleason, H.: *An Introduction to Descriptive Linguistics. Revised edition. New York: Holt,* Rinehart and Winston.

Saporta, S., ed.: *Psycholinguistics.* New York: Holt, Rinehart and Winston.

1963

Eisenson, J., J. Ayer and J. Irwin: Language Development in the Child, in, *The Psychology of Communication.* New York: Appleton-Century-Crofts.

1964

Carroll, J.: *Language and Thought.* Englewood Cliffs: Prentice-Hall.

Fodor, J. and J. Katz., eds.: *The Structure of Language.* Englewood Cliffs: Prentice-Hall.

Lenneberg, E., ed.: *New Directions in the Study of Language.* Cambridge: Michigan Institute of Technology Press.

1965

Jenkins, J.: Mediation Theory and Grammatical Behavior, in, *Directions in Psycholinguistics.* S. Rosenberg, ed., New York: MacMillan.

1966

Brown, R. and U. Bullugi: Three Processes in the Child's Acquisition of Syntax, in *Language and Learning.* J. Emig, J. Fleming and J. Popp, eds., New York: Harcourt, Brace and World.

Emig, J., J. Fleming and J. Popp: *Language and Learning.* New York: Harcourt, Brace and World.

Jakobson, Jr.: Linguistic Types of Aphasia, in *Brain Function, III: Speech, Language and Communication.* University of California at Los Angeles Forum in Medical Sciences, Number 4, Los Angeles: University of California Press.

Kendall, D.: Language and Communication Problems in Children, in, *Speech Pathology.* R. Reiber and R. Brubaker, eds., Amsterdam: North Holland Publishing Company.

Tikofsky, R.: Language Problems in Adults, in, *Speech Pathology*. R. Reiber and R. Brubaker, eds., Amsterdam: North Holland Publishing Company.

1967

Haring N., and R. Schiefelbusch, eds.: *Methods in Special Education*. New York: McGraw-Hill.

Lenneberg, E.: *Biological Foundations of Language*. New York: Wiley. Schiefelbush, R., R. Copeland and J. Smith, eds.: *Language and Mental Retardation*. New York: Holt, Rinehart and Winston.

1968

Deutsch, M., J. Katz and A. Jenson, eds.: *Social Class, Race and Psychological Development*. New York: Holt, Rinehart and Winston.

Dixon, T. and D. Horton, eds.: *Verbal Behavior and General Behavior Theory*. Englewood Cliffs: Prentice-Hall.

Langacker, R.: *Language and Its Structure*. New York: Harcourt, Brace and World.

Rommetveit, R.: *Words, Meanings, and Messages*. New York: Academic Press.

Rosenberg, S., and J. Koplin, eds.: *Developments in Applied Psycholinguistics* Research. New York: MacMillan.

Zale, E., ed.: *Language and Language Behavior*. New York: Appleton-Century-Crofts.

1969

Chomsky, D.: *The Acquisition of Syntax in Children from Five to Ten.* Cambridge: Michigan Institute Technology Press.

1970

McNeill, D.: The Development of Language, in, *The Manual of Child Psychology,* 3rd ed. P. Mussen, ed., New York: Wiley.

1972

Bellugi, U. and R. Brown: *The Aquisition of Language.* Chicago: University of Chicago Press.

Irwin, J. and C. Marge: *Principles of Childhood Language Disabilities.* New York: Appleton-Century Crofts.

Lee, L.: *Developmental Sentence Analysis.* Evanston: Northwestern University Press.

Menyuk, P.: *The Development of Speech.* New York: Bobbs-Merrill.

1973

Brown, R.: *A First Language—The Early Stages.* Cambridge: Harvard University Press.

1974

Schefelbusch, R. and L. Lloyd.: *Language Perspectives—Acquisition, Retardation, and Intervention.* Baltimore: University Park Press.

1975

Lee, L., and R. Koenegsknecht, and S. Mulhern: *Interactive Language Development Teaching.* Evanston: Northwestern University Press.

1976

Schiefelbusch, R.: *The Basis of Language Intervention.* Baltimore: University Park Press.

Audiology

1938

West, R., L. Kennedy and A. Carr: *The Rehabilitation of Speech.* New York: Harper and Brothers, pp. 395-406.

1943

Bunch, C.: *Clinical Audiometry.* Saint Louis: The Mosby Company.

1947

Davis, H: *Hearing and Deafness.* New York: Murray Hill Books.

West, R., L. Kennedy and A. Carr: *The Rehabilitation of Speech.* New York: Harper and Brothers, pp. 546-558.

1948

Johnson, W., *et al.: Speech Handicapped School Children.* New York: Harper Brothers, pp. 366-405.

1949

Dahl, L.: *Public School Audiometry Principles and Methods.* Danville: The Interstate.

Watson, T., and T. Tolan: *Hearing Tests and Hearing Instruments.* New York: Hafner Publishing Company.

1958

Newby, H.: *Audiology: Principles and Practice.* New York: Appleton-Century-Crofts.

1961

Portmann, M., and Portmann, C.: *Clinical Audiometry.* Springfield: Charles C Thomas.

1964

Newby, H.: *Audiology Principles and Practice.* Second Edition. New York: Appleton-Century-Crofts.

1965

Glorig, A.: *Audiometry Principles and Practice.* Baltimore: Williams and Wilkins Company.

1966

O'Neill, J., and H. Oyer: *Applied Audiometry.* New York: Dodd, Mead.

Nober, E., ed. *Audiological Assessment.* Englewood Cliffs: Prentice-Hall.

1972

Katz, J., ed.: *Handbook of Clinical Audiology.* Baltimore: Williams and Wilkins Company.

1973

Holloway, G.: Clinical Audiology, in, *An Appraisal of Speech Pathology and Audiology: A*

Symposium. J. Wingo and G. Holloway, eds., Springfield: Charles C Thomas.

1975

Martin, F.: *Introduction to Audiology*. Englewood Cliffs: Prentice Hall.

CHAPTER III

WRITING THE PAPER

The real value of a research project, whether it be historical, documentary, descriptive or experimental, is to be able to communicate your results as clearly and concisely as possible. One professor once said it neatly: "If you've got information in here (pointing to his head), but can't get it out here (pointing to his mouth) or here (making a writing motion with his hand), it doesn't do anyone, including yourself any good." As previously indicated, the best way yet to be discovered for writing a clear, well-organized paper is to perform a well-organized, planned research project, keeping good notes on everything as it is accomplished. Thus, when the work is done, one merely has to transform his notes into text, elaborating on some points and summarizing others, and, *voila,* the report is done!

The historical or documentary type project usually follows a rather traditional form or plan of organization which differs from the traditional method of writing experimental research reports. The essential elements of both types of reports will be discussed in the next two sections. We hasten to add here a word about these "traditional" methodologies. Traditional methods of writing are not followed merely because they are traditional but rather because long, hard experience by researchers over the years has shown that they work. This fact, after all, is how the methods became traditional.

GENERAL ORGANIZATIONAL SCHEME FOR NON-EXPERIMENTAL RESEARCH REPORTS

Phase 1 - Selecting a Topic

This is a preliminary stage involving the selection of a topic and the location of informational sources. In another section of this book we have already provided you with general survey sources and lists of publications designed to aid in the location of sources. Thus, at least a portion of your job has already been done for you.

Let us say that you have decided to write a paper in speech pathology, and, moreover, you have already scanned through the survey sources and narrowed down the topic to the subject of articulation. It should be clear from your survey review that this topic is far too broad for a single paper of the kind usually required for one class at the undergraduate level (it is, by the way, also too broad for a hefty book at the doctoral level). Within the area of articulation there are many topics which can be researched. A first step is to enumerate, using only a word or two, the possible topics you have been able to discern during your survey reading. For example:

1) The nature of the articulatory process

2) Research methods in studying articulation

3) Theories of causation of articulation problems

4) Incidence and types of articulation problems

5) Treatment of articulation problems, etc.

Assuming that a narrower topic has been selected from this array of topics the next step is to locate potential sources of information about it and to begin the construction of a working bibliography.

Phase 2 - A Working Bibliography

This phase is still preliminary in nature and consists of bringing a list of potential sources to bear on the topic. Each potential source is recorded on a three-by-five card, identifying the source as a book, book chapter, article, research report, etc. The name of the author, title of the work, volume number, date, publisher, and page numbers are also recorded on the card. This process is done for each source, whether or not it will ultimately be used. The title can come from sources such as this book, abstracts, yearly listings of contents of specific journals, and other sources identified in another section of this book. One easy way to get started is to select one of the most recent books on the subject matter and refer to the list of references which usually follow each chapter.

Next, scanning your cards, subdivide them into groups which seem, by their title, to bear on different aspects of your main theme. For example, if you had selected the topic of "Types and Incidence of Articulation Problems," you already have at least two subdivisions: i.e., books, articles, etc., that appear devoted to various *types* of problems, and various survey and study sources related to *incidence.* The titles will often reveal other subdivisions, such as types by primary etiology like "the articulatory patterns of pre- and post-operative cleft palate children," or specific incidences by age and setting such as "the incidence of frontal and lateral lisps in nursery school children."

Phase 3 - Notes

This is the phase where you actually begin to work on the research project proper. One subdivisional group of file cards is selected, and an effort is made to acquire as many of the sources listed on these cards as possible. Each actual source is then scanned for relevant information, and when such information is found, the exact title of the work, including all of the information that was on the three-by-five card, is placed at the top of a five-by-eight card, along with the sub-divisional title and, most importantly, the page numbers. The remainder of the larger card is used to summarize the basic information pertinent to your theme found in a particular work. Other cautions must be observed in taking notes: quotes, secondary sources, paraphrasing, and interpretation.

In quoting an author, extreme care should be exercised, making certain that the quote is exact and that sufficient context for the quote is provided to allay the possibility of the quote being misinterpreted. It should go without saying that a quote must be properly cited.

Secondary sources, i.e., other author's works being cited by the author of the work you are reading, should be clearly identified as secondary sources (preferably, an attempt should be made to secure the original work being cited and refer to it).

When paraphrasing statements made by authors, again one must exercise extreme care to assure that the paraphrased statement reflects as accurately as possible the content and meaning of the author's statement, making certain that your own interpretations are left out.

With regard to personal interpretation, every effort should be made to reveal that such statements are, indeed, subjective interpretations. There are several "lead-in phrases" which make it clear that you are speaking for yourself. Examples are "One might conclude from Jones' articles. . .," "Comparing Jones' and Smith's views, it can be seen that. . .," "The present writer believes. . .," etc.

You may find that you need several five-by-eight cards to get down all the information that is pertinent. Be certain that *each* card contains all of the identifying information as to the source and then merely number the cards sequentially. This is important and is drawn to your attention because it is disasterous to have dozens of cards fall on the floor or in some other way get out of order with no easy way to restore them.

Each subdivisional group of smaller working bibliography cards should be researched in the above manner. Frequently, you will notice that your subdivisional categories will change as dictated by the actual information you are reading. *Allow* these changes to occur. Remember your original subdivision scheme was based upon what could be gleaned from reviewing titles. New subdivisional schemes will have at their basis knowledge which you are acquiring by the process of your research. In other words, organization based on knowledge if preferable to organization based on guesswork.

Phase 4 - Outlines

This phase involves organizing the information you have acquired relative to your theme in ways that will allow for a logical outline to be followed in the writing of the paper.

A good beginning is to translate your general theme, "Types and Incidence of Articulation Problems," into a statement of purpose. The subdivisions that finally evolved in preparing your five-by-eight cards should aid you in creating this statement of purpose. An example might be, "The purpose of this paper is to describe the ten basic kinds of articulation problems, the rationale for their categorization, and their incidence in the general population and certain sub-populations."

Next comes the construction of a sentence outline, an organizational scheme for accomplishing your stated purposes, allowing you to transfer the information from your cards to textual material which will be logical and clear in its presentation. Below is one possible outline.

I. Types of articualtion problems.
   A. Categorization by faulty place of articulation.

B. Categorization by faulty manner of articulation.
C. Categorization by voiced sounds versus unvoiced sounds.
D. Categorization by etiology.
   1. Functional articulation problems.
      a. Faulty learning.
      b. Breakdown theories.
      c. Transient perceptual problems.
      d. etc.
   2. Articulation problems secondary to other conditions.
      a. Cerebral palsy.
      b. Cleft palate.
      c. Cerebral-vascular accident.
      d. Mental retardation.
      e. etc.

II. Incidence.
A. How information is gathered.
   1. Surveys - physicians, hospitals, clinics, schools, etc.
   2. Large samples.
      a. Thousands of people at the 1939 World's Fair.
      b. Longitudinal study of articulation paterns of five thousand Minneapolis school children.
      c. etc.
B. Present compilation and reporting of incidence-obtained from the type of sources outlined in II-A.
   1. Incidence figures by categorizations outlined in I.
   2. Provide ranges as well as averages.
   3. etc.

III. Summary and Conclusions.
   A. What can be learned from the above information - how is it useful?
      1. Reveals the scope of the problem.
      2. Implications for manpower needs in speech pathology.
      3. Implications for pure and applied research, prevention, early identification, etc.
   B. Critique of the quality and quanity of information.
      1. Lack of categorization agreement among various authors.
      2. Lack of uniformity of vocabulary.
      3. Wide disparity among incidence figures by various authors.
      4. Lack of truly current figures.
      5. etc.

The outline presented above is not intended to be a model or ideal. The actual outline is going to be determined by the subdivisional categories established on your five-by-eight cards.

Phase 5 - Writing the Report

This is the final phase of the report. Essentially it involves translating the outline into textual form, using the information, quotes, paraphrasing, and commentery already existing on your file cards. The best way to begin is to sit down armed with the following aids: your original three-by-five cards, your five-by-eight cards, your outline, a dictionary, a thesaurus and a writing guide such as you are reading. Remember, your task now is to place the information you have on paper so you may clearly and logically transmit the information you have gathered to others.

Aside from grammatical form the mechanics of writing which presents the most difficulty to students is related to the use of footnote and bibliography. A detailed review with examples is provieded in appendix A.

This last phase of the writing project usually requires several drafts, smoothing out sentence structure, arriving at final headings and subheadings, making certain the document is paragraphed properly, and that there are good transition sentences linking each successive paragraph to the one before it. Many have found the "cut and paste" approach of value. After the first rough draft has been prepared, simply cut up the paper and rearrange sentences, paragraphs, and sections by rearranging the cut-up draft. After having done so, paste them together. Surprisingly, one often saves a great deal of time by following this approach. It allows the writer to observe the continuity of various arrangements without having to rewrite. Try it. We think you will agree.

Presented below is an actual paper written by a student as a research project of the non-experimental variety. The paper was one of the student's early graduate writing assignments and was not written with any intent of publication.

There have been alterations in the paper for purposes of illustration. The original referencing system has been changed from referencing within the text to footnotes (see Appendix A). Many of the errors contained within the paper have been inserted by the authors to serve our purpose. The changes have been made with knowledge and permission of the student who prepared the paper.

THE SEX RATIO IN STUTTERING

by

Elaine Jackle Taylor

A Paper Presented
in Partial Fulfillment
of the Course Requirements for
Stuttering: Theories and Therapies

Summer Quarter

INTRODUCTION

We really ought to find out why children stutter. The answer may be found in the persistent sex ratio difference. As of now, this may be the only difference that continues to make a difference.[1]

There has been one outstanding and persistent finding concerning the prevalence of stuttering which is in complete agreement by all authorities. Although different researchers have reported different ratios, it is commonly accepted that male stutterers outnumber female stutterers three to four to one.[2]

Why this great disparity between the number of males and females affected? While one would expect to find an abundance of material offering some explanation, there has not been a great amount of research conducted to investigate the relationship of the sex ratio to the etiology of the stuttering disorder. The information which is available was obtained by studies completed over a decade ago, and this material, in most cases, has been proven inconclusive or invalid by more research. This lack of information is surprising when one considers the amount of space devoted to stuttering in the professional journals. Nonetheless,

---

[1]Jon Eisenson: Observations of the Incidence of Stuttering in a Special Culture, *ASHA*, VII-VIII (1965-1966), 391-394.

[2]Charles Van Riper: *The Nature of Stuttering, (Englewood Cliffs, New Jersey: Prentice-Hall, Inc., 1971).*

there are several interesting facts unique to the sex ratio in stuttering that may be worth mentioning at this time.

(1) Although it is generally accepted that male stutterers tend to outnumber female stutterers about three to four to one, different researchers have reported varying ratios. Mills and Streit[3] found a ratio of 5:1 in a speech survey conducted in Holyoke, Massachusetts: whereas, Dickson reported a ratio of only 2:1 in a survey of American school children in 1969.[4]

Schuell lists several factors which seem to contribute to this variation in reported ratios.

(1) Method of survey. (a) Data yielded by questionnaires are supplied by individuals whose knowledge of, and whose definition of stuttering may differ widely. (b) Data yielded by survey procedures and criteria of stuttering held by different examiners, and by the ability of some stutterers to escape detection in a short interview.

HE USE
F THE
AME
NUMERA-
ION IN
OTH THE
AJOR
ND
UBTOPIC
S
ONFUSING

THE FOOTNOTE NUMBER SHOULD FOLLOW THE PASSAGE TO WHICH IT REFERS

DICKSON APPEARS TO BE A SECONDARY SOURCE. THE FOOTNOTE SHOULD SO INDICATE

[3]A. Mills and H. Streit, "Report of a Speech Survey in Holyoke, Massachusetts", *Journal of Speech and Hearing Disorders,* VII (1942), 165.

[4]Van Riper, *op. cit.*

PAGE NUMBER SHOULD BE PROVIDED

It is also acceptable to drop *op. cit.* or *loc. cit.* and use only the author's surname, an abbreviation of the title, and page reference, as:

Van Riper, *Nature of Stuttering,* p. 142.

This method makes the cited work more readily identifiable and any additional information desired by the reader may be found in the bibliography. As you read through this paper the value of the abbreviated method will become obvious.

Enumerations are frequently improperly presented by the student, thus creating confusion. A correct outline form follows:

1. Male stutterers tend. . .
   A. Reported ratios vary
      1. Factors which contribute. . .
         a. Method of survey
            i) Date obtained from. . .
            ii) Date may be influenced by. . .
         b. Age of stutterers observed
         c. Certain selective factors
            i) Factors which operate after the compulsory school age is reached
            ii) Factor of severity of stuttering

It appears that in this particular case the confusion may be resolved by not enumerating the "... several interesting facts. . ."

(2) Age of stutterers observed. The ratio of male to female stutterers varies with age level.

(3) Selective factors operating in populations studied. (a) In school populations a selective factor operates after the age of compulsory school attendance. (b) In surveys based on stutterers referred for clinical treatment, the data are probably influenced by the severity of stuttering and the degree of maladjustment experienced because of stuttering, since the majority of those who experience only a mild degree of difficulty probably do not seek clinical help . . .[5]

Van Riper lists another reason why the true proportion is in some doubt. He feels that ". . . most of the investigations of the sex ratio in stuttering fail to take into account the ratio of total male to female populations from which the samples were obtained."[6]

In spite of all the limitations of the investigations, there is no report to date which indicates that more females than males stutter.

(2) Another persistent finding concerning the sex ratio is the consistency in the reports from other cultures, which vary widely in their child-rearing practices. Eisenson found the usual ratio among

---

[5]Hildred Schuell, "Sex Differences in Relation to Stuttering Part I.", *Journal of Speech and Hearing Disorders,* XI (1946), 281.

[6]Van Riper, *op. cit.* p. 170

the children in an Israeli kibutzim, despite the similarity in treatment of boys and girls from early infancy through early adolescence.[7] Aaron found a ratio of 3.28 males to 1 female who stuttered in the Bantu tribe of South Africa, where child-rearing practices are vastly different when compared to those in the American culture.[8]

(3) The third fact is in some dispute among various authors. This is the hypothesis that the sex ratio varies with the age level.

CANNOT B[E] CALLED A FACT IF IT IS IN DISPUTE AND ALS[O] A HYPOTHES[IS]

Schuell reported the ratio of male-female rises steadily with age until adulthood is reached, and that the ratio was found to be higher among the university group than in the non-university group of the same age level.[9] This may be due to the fact that male stutterers are more motivated to acquire university education in spite of their handicap. However, Mills and Streit were unable to find any change in the ratio with reference to grade placement.[10]

(4) One cannot conclude this section without mentioning the obvious-the fact that males outnumber females in many other types of deviancies and disorders. Van Riper lists Chorea, asthma, convulsions, tetany,

---

[7]Eisenson, *op. cit.*, pp. 391-394.

[8]Myrtle Aron, "The Nature and Incidence of Stuttering Among a Bantu Group of School-going Children", *Journal of Speech and Hearing Disorders,* XXVII (1962), 116-128.

[9]Schuell, *op. cit.*, pp. 277-298.

[10]Mills and Streit, *op. cit.*, pp. 161-167.

and epilepsy as only some of the spasmodic disorders which could be cited. Baldness, cleft palate, and spinal bifida are just a few of the many other disorders where males outnumber females.[11] Schuell reports more male than female stillborns and more risk of birth injuries to the male child as he is usually larger than the female child at birth.[12]

The male population appears to be more susceptible to stress and related physiological involvements-ulcers, high-blood pressure and cardiac involvements. Generally, males enjoy a shorter life span than females.

Unfortunately, these facts do not prove very useful in helping us to determine the reason behind the sex ratio in stuttering. Furthermore, this ratio is reportedly much higher than for any of the above disorders.

Several theories have been advanced in the attempt to explain the greater vulnerability of males to stuttering. I will attempt to review some of the more important studies completed in this area. It must be noted that there are differing points of view represented with respect to the nature and etiology of this disorder, and this naturally affects the conclusions thus drawn about the sex ratio. Many of the theories listed consider a composite view. For example, Karlin's "psychoso-

---

[11]Van Riper, *op. cit.,* p. 137.

[12]Schuell, *op. cit.,* pp. 277-298.

matic theory" is based upon organic and psychological factors. Some of the others-Mysak, Schuell, and Bloodstein-incorporate environmental, cultural and parental factors in their research and conclusions. For expediency, the chosen studies will be discussed under two broad categories; physiological and environmental.

The introduction should serve as an orientation to the paper. In the introduction the student has presented the nature of the problem and has reviewed related studies. The review of the literature has pointed out the issues involved and reveals the importance of each to the theme. We can conclude that the student has a good introduction.

PHYSIOLOGICAL FACTORS

Flechsig was one of the first investigators to propose a possible explanation for the sex ratio in stuttering. He found that myelinization occurs earlier in the female than in the male.[13]

Most of the nerve fibers of the central nervous system are invested with a myelin sheath that is regarded as having an insulating func-

[13]P. Flechsig, *Meine Myelogenetische Hernlehre.* (Berlin: Julius Springer, 1927) Cited by Isaac Karlin, "A Psychosomatic Theory of Stuttering," *Journal of Speech and Hearing Disorders,* XII (1947), 319-322.

tion. This myelinization is usually positively correlated with function. For example, a nerve fiber that has not been completely myelinated may transmit impulses but the resulting action will lack precision and fine coordination. Conduction is also slower among amyelinated nerve fibers.

Flechsig also noted that myelinization may not be complete until the twentieth year of life. Furthermore, although a normally developed cortex is essential for the symbolic reception and expression of speech, complete myelinization of the speech areas is a comparatively late process in cortical development.

ADVANCED WOULD APPEAR TO BE THE BETTER CHOICE IN THIS CASE

Another physiological factor which might support the sex ratio in stuttering was forwarded by Palmer and Martin and Gillet. These authors found a difference in the cardiac rhythms of stutterers and non-stutterers. Whereas, the pulse rhythm decreases in irregularity with increase in age in normal subjects, the stutterers' cardiac rhythms increase in irregularity. This was found true for both sexes; however, the larger increases in irregularity in the male stutterers was significant.[14]

This, the authors concluded, the cause of stuttering must be sought

[14]Palmer, Martin and A. M. Gillett, "Sex Differences in the Cardiac Rhythm of Stutterers," *Journal of Speech and Hearing Disorders,* III (1938), 7-12.

in a sex-linked metabolic picture. They felt that neither increased heart rate, nor increased irregularity of heartbeat are necessarily direct causes of stuttering, but are a part of a direct by-effect of a sex linked mechanism causing stuttering.

WHY IS IT NEEDLESS TO SAY?

Needless to say, this discovery enjoyed a brief and nondescript history, and it appears that no further studies were conducted to expand this theory.

The phrase "needless to say" is superfluous in this situation. One should use no more words than are necessary to ensure clarity. Consider this re-writing:". . .sex linked mechanism causing stuttering. This discovery enjoyed a brief and nondescript history."

UP TO THIS POINT THE WRITER HAS USED LAST NAMES ONLY. ONE SHOULD BE CONSISTANT

Isaac W. Karlin, incorporating the earlier views of Flechsig, also proposed that the primary or basic cause of stuttering is a dealy in the myelinization of the stressful period around the age of three, he will be more susceptible to stuttering. If this emotional stress is lessened, the child's speech will improve, while time is allowed for myelinization to develop. If the stuttering continues, emotional factors will begin to play a greater and greater role in maintaining or perpetuating the disorder.[15]

Morley experimentally confirmed the differences in central laterality of stutterers and non-stutterers, as suggested by the dominance theory and offered an explanation for the greater incidence of stuttering in males. Electro-encephalograms were obtained from a stuttering and non-stuttering population. The research was based on the belief that the percentage of the alpha rhythm that was present might be related negatively to what is termed as 'cortical excitatory state.' Stimulation which

The transition between the two paragraphs is too abrupt. A smoother flow of ideas from the previous paragraph is desirable.

Need double quotation marks

Primary quotations that are long enough to be single-spaced and indented replace double quotation marks at the beginning and end of the quote. If a quotation is made within a quotation, single quotation marks are used. For a short quote, double quotation marks are used.

should lead to an increased excitatory state should, therefore, cause a decrease in the percentage time of alpha rhythm present. The findings showed that the percentage time the alpha rhythm was present during silence was usually greater in the non-dominant hemisphere. Stutterers tended to have a higher percentage time of alpha present in the left than in the right occipital

[15]Isaac W. Karlin, "A Psychosomatic Theory of Stuttering." *Journal of Speech And Hearing Disorders*. xii, (1949), 319-322.

areas, although no significant difference was found between the right and left motor areas. This suggests that there is a higher incidence of left-sided cerebral dominance in stutterers.

Thus, Morley concludes, it is reasonable to suggest that there may be an inherent tendency in males towards a delay in the stabilization of the neuromuscular patterns of speech associated with lack of definite right-sided laterality and dominant left cerebral hemisphere.[16]

One should avoid the use of such qualifiers

ENVIRONMENTAL FACTORS

Probably one of the most prominent and thorough investigations regarding the sex difference in stuttering was completed by Schuell. Her two-part study has been widely quoted and has stimulated further research.

Strunk and White refer to qualifiers as ". . .leeches that infest the pond of prose, sucking the blood of words."[1]

The use of "probably" adds nothing to the sentence, and tends to weaken the value of the cited study.

[1]William Strunk and E. B. White. *The Elements of Style,* 2nd ed. New York: MacMillan Co., 1972, p. 65.

---

[16]Muriel Morley, *The Development and Disorders of Speech in Childhood,* (Baltimore: The Williams and Wilkins Company, 1965), 147.

Schuell began her investigation by studying related areas where a sex difference could be found. Aside from the sex difference in mortality, disease and physical growth, she found that the rate of development of language was more accelerated for girls than for boys after the first year. The magnitude of the difference in favor of the girls tended to increase with age, and girls were slightly ahead of boys in the age at which they begin to use meaningful words. Boys tended to make more articulatory errors than girls, and there was a tendency for boys to outnumber girls in the cases of speech retardation.

When Schuell investigated the area of mental growth and school achievement, she found that girls tended to excel on tests which had a verbal element, from the age of school entrance through adolescence.[17]

In regard to sex differences in behavior problems and maladjustments, Schuell reported a study by Stodgill.[18] He found that parents and teachers tended to approve of child behavior which made for smooth running of household and classroom, and to show little regard for withdrawn, self-centered reactions. Clinical psychologists, on the other hand, tended to

---

[17]Schuell, *op. cit.* pp. 277-298.

[18]R. M. Stodgill, "Attitudes of Parents, Students and Mental Health Hygienists Towards Children's Behavior," *Journal of Social Psychology,* IV (1933), 486-489. Cited by Part I," *Journal of Speech and Hearing Disorders,* XI (1946), 277-298.

approve of active, extroverted social adjustment in children, regardless of parent and teacher convenience. This is only one of the many contradictory attitudes prevalent in our culture.

Reporting studies from a secondary source can be difficult. The most desirable approach is to gain the information from the original if possible. If the original source cannot be obtained, the interpretation of the original by the secondary report should be indicated. Thus, the text should read:

Schuell reported a study by Stodgill.[19] According to Schuell, he found. . .

Thus, Schuell concluded, a tenable hypothesis would seem to be that the male child, whose physical, social and language development proceeds at a slower rate than that of the female, encounters more unequal competition and consequently more frustration, particularly in relation to language situations and that as a result, he exhibits more insecurity, more hesitancy and more inhibitions in speech.

Furthermore, if the frustrating situations are too many, if his speech behavior is compared unfavorable reaction to it on the part of other people, it is conceivable that the anxieties, tensions and the overt

[19]Hildred Schuell, "Sex Differences in Relations to Stuttering," *Journal of Speech and Hearing Disorders,* XVI (1947), 23-38.

behavior regarded as stuttering might develop.

Schuell further explains that the contradictory attitudes prevalent in our culture would tend to increase tensions and frustrations in the male child. First, it is demanded of the male child that he exhibit independence, fearlessness, self-control and a certain amount of aggressiveness; second, that he must at the same time be submissive, orderly, and obedient. His behavior must not disturb the order and routine of home or classroom, and it must conform to standards of parents and teachers.

In Part II of her study, Schuell administered informal questionnaires to a group of fifth, sixth, seventh and eighth graders in order to evaluate the children's reactions to the typothesized sex differences in the attitudes of parents and teachers. The data seemed to imply that girls felt more security than boys in family, school and social situations. They appeared to be more sheltered than boys who were encouraged to be dependent, were praised more and punished less severely. They appeared to encounter less conflict in the total environment. Boys in the same age groups, who tended to be less mature physically, mentally, and socially, seemed to be forced into sterner competitions and were handled less gently than girls. They were punished for the same types of aggressive behaviors that they were forced to develop in order to compete with girls, hold their own with boys, compete in school and sports, and eventually as a wage-earner in socicty.[20]

The inequality of treatment between young males and females is evident in our culture. Pufall lists several such inequalities:

(1) Girls may cry; boys may not. If girls cry, they are consoled; if boys cry, they are reprimanded.

(2) "Tomboy" versus "sissy." The male child is not permitted the range of freedom the female child is permitted.

(3) Girls may more readily show affection for one another than boys may.

(4) Girls may hit boys; boys do not hit girls. Girls may stand up to boys; boys are "bullies" if they stand up to girls.

(5) Girls report, inform, are mothers' helpers when they tell on little boys' misbehavior; little boys are "tattle-tales."

(6) Girls may wear boys' clothing; boys may not wear girls' clothing.

(7) Girls may play boys' games or use boys' toys; boys may not play with girls' toys.

(8) Boys competing with girls can't win; if he wins, there is no victory because this is expected of him; if he doesn't win, he is scorned, laughed at or teased.

---

[20] *Ibid.*

(9) Boys should be, are expected to be, stronger, faster, and quicker than girls. This is a terrible mis-conception, especially when the girl is neurologically and physically ahead of the boy in rate of development.

(10) Girls may be hugged, held, petted and fonded; boys are not. This can have tremendous psychological implications.

(11) Girls should be, and are encouraged to be 'little girls'; boys should be 'little men'.[21]

The above paragraph indicates the complexity of referencing. In this case, the information presented is a paraphrase of lecture material. It is presented, however, as if it is a direct quote, i.e., it is idented and single-spaced. An acceptable approach is to change the wording slightly (Pufall[21] discusses. . .) and enumerate the inequalities as part of the textual discussion without indentation or single-spacing.

The evidence is incriminating. It appears that a re-examination and revision of some of the assumptions upon which our more prevalent forms of educational and social theory are based is necessary.

In conclusion, Schuell states "that stuttering and the sex difference in the incidence of stuttering can be accounted for by a combina-

[21]Harold Pufall, Class Lectures, Stuttering: Theories and Therapies, June 19-23, 1972.

tion of psychologically determined factors and responses to culturally-determined stimulus-complexes which are different for girls and boys, for men and women."[22]

However, the evidence on which Schuell rests her conclusions leaves something to be desired. Van Riper feels that her subject group was inadequate, that her "subjects were taken from the fifth to seventh grades-far later than the age at which stuttering generally begins. Her questions seem inappropriately designed to elicit significant information regarding communicative pressures and no reliability check was made."[23]

One simple way to test Schuell's hypothesis could be to examine other cultures in regard to treatment of children during their years of speech development. As explained previously, two authors, Eisenson and Aron, found a comparable ratio of male to female stutterers in Israeli kibbutzim and in the Bantu tribe of South Africa, respectively.[24&25]

---

[23]Van Riper, *op. cit.* p. 142.

[24]Eisenson, *op. cit.,* p. 392.

[25]Aron, *op. cit.* pp. 116-128.

The use of phraseology such as: "as explained earlier" or "as previously mentioned" rather commonly appears in early reports written by students. It usually results in an awkward and lengthy sentence. Consider this alternative:

> The investigations of Eisenson[24] and Aron[25] revealed a comparable ratio of male to female stutterers in both Israeli kibbutzim and in the Bantu tribe of South Africa.

In the Israeli kibbutzim, the children are separated from their parents at a very early age and are raised in communal dorms. There are not conscious differences in the treatment of the children along sex lines. Nonetheless, a ratio of three to four boys: one girl was reported. In contrast, Aron found the young Bantu child to be greatly indulged, and the relationship between mother and child to be both affectionate and close. The period of lactation sometimes extends up to three years, at which time this is suddenly brought to an end by way of various rituals. The mother then ceases to have the child in close proximity to her, and demonstrations of affection are not encouraged. After weaning, the child's socialization increases rapidly as he is thrust into the company of other children. Despite this variation in child-rearing practices, Aron reported a ratio of 3.28:1.

Mysak also attempted to clarify the cultural implications relative to the sex ratio. He felt two obvious explanations presented themselves when one examined the sex ratio on the basis of Johnson's "diagnosogenic" theory:

(1) The possibility that boys, may, in actuality, be less fluent than girls and, consequently, more prone to misdiagnosis.

(2) The possibility that males may be exposed to higher standards of fluency because of our particular society and are, consequently, more frequently diagnosed as stutterers.[26]

Mysak attempted to discover whether a sex difference in standards of fluency existed among adolescent boys and girls. He found that adolescent girls made significantly more diagnoses of stuttering than boys, and that older adolescent boys made slightly fewer diagnoses of stuttering. Thus, from this data, it appears that the sex ratio can be more easily explained in terms of an actual difference in fluency, per se, existing in an atmosphere of high standards of fluency for both sexes.

Bloodstein and Smith also attempted to determine whether we actually have higher standards of fluency for boys than girls, on the hypothesis that this would be a contributing cause to the sex ratio in stuttering.

---

[26]Edward Mysak, "Diagnosis of Stuttering as Made by Adolescent Boys and Girls," *Journal of Speech and Hearing Disorders,* XXIV (1959), p. 30.

The object of their study was to determine how far non-fluency is tolerated in the speech of boys and girls as measured by the readiness with which normal children of either sex are diagnosed as stutterers adults. College students listened to samples of sexually ambiguous speech recordings. The results showed that boys were regarded as stutterers slightly more often than girls by both male and female students, but the results were insignificant. The authors concluded that the sex ratio in stuttering is due to factors other than a difference in cultural standards of fluency for male and female.[27]

Perhaps more important to the sex difference is stuttering than cultural standards is parental attitude, or the parent-child relationships. A number of studies deal with parental attitudes and their influence upon personality development. In the field of speech pathology there have been a few attempts to measure parental attitudes in the etiology of stuttering.

Bloodstein, Jaeger Tureen found that parents of stutterers made a larger number of diagnoses of stuttering than a group of parents of non-stutterers. The inference can be drawn that these parents have rather high expectations regarding the fluency of their children and are

[27]Oliver Bloodstein and Sonja Smith, "A Study of the Diagnosis of Stuttering with Special Reference to the Sex Ratio," *Journal of Speech and Hearing Disorders,* XIX (1954), 459-466.

consequently inclined to react to them as stutterers more readily than the average parent. The crucial implication of this finding is that the extent to which a child's non-fluency is excessive or conspicuous is determined by the amount of repetition in his speech, but also, to a significant degree, by who is listening.[28]

What appears even more crucial in the parent-child relationship is the presence of covert, rather than overt, rejection. Kinstler mathced an experimental group of thirty mothers of young male stutterers to a control group of thirty mothers of normal children for age, education, size of family, age of children, socioeconomic status, religion, psychological guidance, and education of spouses. Both groups were administered a projective-type questionnaire designed to measure covert rejection, overt rejection, covert acceptance, and overt acceptance. The results yielded significant differences in the patterns of responses.

(a) Mothers of young male stutterers reject their children convertly far more, but overtly far less than do the mothers of normal speakers.

(b) Mothers of stutterers accept their children covertly less, and

[28]Oliver Bloodstein, William Jaeger and Jack Tureen, "A Study of the Diagnosis of Stuttering by Parents of Stutterers and Non-Stutterers," *Journal of Speech and Hearing Disorders,* XVII (1952), 308-315.

overtly only slightly less, than do mothers of normal speakers.

(c) Mothers of stutterers reject their children more than they accept them; while mothers of normal speakers accept their children more than reject them.[29]

Kinstler explains that clinical observations based upon individual and group psychotherapy with stutterers seem to suggest that one of the strongest feelings of many stutterers is the feeling of hidden or covert rejection by the mother.

It is not surprising that overt rejection would not be as emotionally damaging to the child as covert rejection. The child would be only too aware of the problem and would be able to act out and express his frustrations without guilt. He would likely react by openly hating his parents for their unfair behavior. The child who is rejected covertly has no legitimate of justifiable outlet for his frustrations. For although his parents do not give love, they may pretend to be acting in the child's best interest and may even be over-protective. As a result, the child will be constantly frustrated. He may be afraid to express his hostilities for fear of further endangering his relationship with his parents. He tries hard to be good,

[29]Donald Kinstler, "Covert and Overt Maternal Rejection in Stuttering," *Journal of Speech and Hearing Disorders,* XXVI (1961), 145-155.

and being good means repressing his aggressive feelings. As speech is a vehicle for the expression of his feelings, he must withhold it. This may eventually result in a partial involuntary withholding of speech, or stuttering.

This pattern of parent-child relationship has also been studied by McCarthy. In her report, she mentions that some children who find themselves in such a hostile world develop a "basic anxiety." These children may withdraw into mutism or attempt to retaliate against the hostile environment, becoming aggressive and hyperactive.[30]

McCarthy also mentions some of the dangers involved when the mother is smothering or overprotective. She feels that these mothers are tense, perfectionistic parents, whose overprotectiveness is often a disguise for a real rejecting attitude. These children may become so ambivalent, that they may even be able to leave home as adults despite of the severe hostility they feel towards their parents.

McCarthy also quotes a study by Moncur. When he compared forty-eight stutterers five to eight years of age with a matched control group, he found that every stuttering child

There is a problem here. Can you identi[fy] it? HINT: See page

[30]Dorothea McCarthy, "Language Disorders and Parent-Child Relationships," *Journal of Speech and Hearing Disorders,* XIX (December, 1954), 514-523.

exhibited several symptoms of maladjustment in addition to his speech problem. He also found that significantly more of the mothers of the stutterers employed harsh disciplinary measures, threat, shame or corporal punishment. They also admitted more inconsistency in discipline and more conflict with the father over discipline.

Yet they still tended to be more indulgent and pampering, especially in regard to eating habits.[31]

Glasner also found that stuttering children frequently have a long background of overprotection, pampering and overanxious, obsessively perfectionistic parents.[32]

Moncur concluded that there appears to be a syndrome of environmental factors which seems to precipitate or aggravate stuttering with significant regularity. This syndrome is a variety of dominating parental actions which include domination by disciplinary action, domination by over-supervising and over-protecting the child, domination by holding the child to excessively high standards and dom-

[31]John Moncur, "Environmental Factors Differentiating Stuttering Children from Non-Stuttering Children," *Speech Monographs*, XVIII (1951), 312-325. Cited by Dorothea McCarthy, "Language Disorders and Parent-Child Relationships," *Journal of Speech and Hearing Disorders*, XIX (December, 1954), 514-523.

[32]Philip Glasner, "Personality Characteristics and Emotional Problems in Stutterers Under the Age of Five," *Journal of Speech and Hearing Disorders*, XIV (1949), 135-138.

ination by adverse parental criticism.[33]

Pufall also mentions several parental factors which would negatively affect the male child more than the female child.

(1) Dominant mother figure and submissive father figure.

(2) A female-oriented mother, thus resulting in a possible covert rejection of the male child.

(3) A female-oriented father, also resulting in a possible covert rejection of the male child.

(4) Unhealthy past relationship between mother and another male, which may lead her to displace her old emotions into her male child.

(5) Unhealthy relationship between mother and husband, with the resulting negative feelings and attitudes, displaced onto the male child.

(6) A father unable to express and/or demonstrate his love to the male child.

(7) The father holding too high standards for his son.

(8) Father unable to accept the son as he is; when aptitudes, interests, skills and personality differ.

(9) Parents, especially father, "too busy" in community, social, civic or political affairs.

(10) Both parents critical, harsh, cold, demanding, or holding too-high standards.

---

[33]John Moncur, "Parental Domination in Stuttering," *Journal of Speech and Hearing Disorders*, XVII (1952), 155-165.

(11) One or both parents overprotective.[34]

Despite the amount of material available, there is an obvious need for further research as specific findings are relatively lacking. The explanation of the sex difference in stuttering remains as obscure as the nature and etiology of the disorder itself. Perhaps the difficulty lies, not in the fact that the sex ratio is difficult to account for, but in the fact that it can be explained on the basis of practically any of the theories of stuttering.

BIBLIOGRAPHY

Aron, Myrtle, L. "The Nature and Incidence of Stuttering Among a Bantu Group of Schoolgoing Children," Journal of Speech and Hearing Disorders, XXVII (1962), 116-128.

Bloodstein, Oliver; Jaeger, William; and Tureen, Jack. "A Study of the Diagnosis of Stuttering by Parents of Stutterers and Non-Stutterers," Journal of Speech and Hearing Disorders, XVII (1952), 308-315.

Bloodstein, Oliver and Smith, Sonja M. "A Study of the Diagnosis of Stuttering with Special Reference to the Sex Ratio," Journal of Speech and Hearing Disorders, XIX (1954), 459-466.

[34] Pufall, *op. cit.*

Eisenson, Jon. "Observations of the Incidence of Stuttering in a Special Culture," ASHA, VII-VIII (1965-1966), 391-394.

Flechsig, P. Meine Myelogenetische Hernlehre, Berlin: Julius Springer, 1927. Cited by Karlin, Isaac, "A Psychosomatic Theory of Stuttering," Journal of Speech and Hearing Disorders, XII (1947), 319-322.

Glasner, Philip J. "Personality Characteristics and Emotional Problems in Stutterers Under the Age of Five," Journal of Speech and Hearing Disorder, XIV (1949), 135-138.

Karlin, Isaac W. "A Psychosomatic Theory of Stuttering," Journal of Speech and Hearing Disorders, XII (1947), 319-322.

Kinstler, Donald B. "Covert and Overt Maternal Rejection in Stuttering," Journal of Speech and Hearing Disorders, XXVI (May, 1961), 145-155.

McCarthy, Dorothea. "Language Disorders and Parent-Child Relationships," Journal of Speech and Hearing Disorders, XIX (December, 1954), 514-523.

Mills, A. and Stret, H. "Report of a Speech Survey in Holyoke, Massachusetts," Journal of Speech and Hearing Disorders, VII (1942), 161-167.

Moncur, John P. "Environmental Factors Differentiating Stuttering Children from Non-Stuttering Children," Speech Monographs, XVIII (1951), 312-325. Cited by McCarthy, Dorothea. "Language Disorders and Parent-Child Relationships," Journal of Speech and Hearing Disorders, XIX (December, 1954), 514-523.

Moncur, John P. "Parental Domination in Stuttering," Journal of Speech and Hearing Disorders, XVII (1952), 155-165.

Morley, Muriel. The Development and Disorders of Speech in Childhood, Baltimore: The Williams and Wilkins Company, 1965.

Mysak, Edward. "Diagnosis of Stuttering as Made by Adolescent Boys and Girls," Journal of Speech and Hearing Disorders, XXIV (1959), 29-33.

Palmer, Martin and Gillett, A.M. "Sex Differences in the Cardiac Rhythm of Stutterers," Journal of Speech and Hearing Disorders, III (1938), 7-12.

Pufall, Harold E. Class Lectures: Stuttering: Theories and Therapies, June 19-23, 1972.

Schuell, Hildred. "Sex Differences in Relation to Stuttering: Part I,"

Journal of Speech and Hearing Disorders, XI (1946), 277-298.

Schuell, Hildred. "Sex Differences in Relation to Stuttering," Journal of Speech and Hearing Disorders, XVI (1947), 23-38.

Stodgill, R. M. "Attitudes of Parents, Students and Mental Health Hygienists Towards sic Children's Behavior," Journal of Social Psychology, IV (1933), 486-489. Cited by Schuell, Hildred. "Sex Differences in Relation to Stuttering: Part I," Journal of Speech and Hearing Disorders, XI (1946), 277-298.

Van Riper, Charles. The Nature of Stuttering, Englewood Cliffs, New Jersey: Prentice-Hall, Incorporated, 1971.

GENERAL ORGANIZATIONAL SCHEME FOR EXPERIMENTAL RESEARCH REPORTS

As indicated earlier, the experimental research report traditionally differs from the non-experimental report. Most of the advice given relative to the non-experimental report is, however, generally valid for the experimental report also. In other words, the use of the three-by-five working bibliography cards is still recommended, and the use of five-by-eight note cards is still recommended. The chief difference lies in the fact that the organizational outline and final form of presentation is dictated by rather stringent rules. There is, of course, another major difference in that the results being reported represent the outcome of an actual carried out experiment, rather than information supplied by other authors and scholars.

With regard to the reporting of experimental research, the professions of speech pathology and audiology have borrowed heavily from the methods proposed by and carried out by our colleagues in the field of experimental psychology. Their method of reporting is almost universally accepted and used by psychologists and is often referred to as the "APA style" (APA standing for American Psychological Association). An elaborate manual has been prepared detailing, with great specificity, this style of reporting.[1]

This specificity is extreme to the point of detailing even the type of punctuation that must

[1]For copies of the APA style manual the student is referred to the American Psychological Association, 1200 17th Northwest, Washington, D.C. 20036

be used in bibliographical references. Speech pathologists and audiologists have evolved a reporting scheme based upon the "APA style" but considerably less stringent and so is often referred to as "modified APA style." Presented below are the essential elements of this reporting style.

I. *Title* - It is essential that titles of experiments should very clearly express the nature of the experiment. With regard to titles, terseness is often not of the essence. In other words, the title should reveal to the potential reader as much information as possible about the nature of the experiment to be described. Therefore, lengthy titles are not deemed to be inappropriate or in bad taste. A few examples are: "Interrelationships Among Oral Breath Pressure Ratios and Articulation Skills for Individuals with Cleft Palate," "Real Ear Versus Artificial Mastoid Methods of Calibration of Bone-Conduction Vibrators," "Frequency, Duration, and Perceptual Measures in Relations to Judgments of Alaryngeal Speech Acceptability," etc.

II. *Statement of the Problem* - This is a brief and to-the-point statement of the purpose of the experiment, the working hypothesis which is being tested or the question which is being posed. Examples might be: "Is there a significant difference between the motor skills of stutters and non-stutters?" "Are there differences in hearing test results between the ascending method of measurement, the descending method of measurement, and bracketing method of measurement"? etc.

III. *Review of the Literature* - Next is a rather lengthy section which purports to review all or most of the pertinent literature relative to the knowledge which already exists which may have a bearing on the posed problem. Here is where the methods described in the section on non-experimental reports come in handy. In essence, this section not only provides information about the current status of knowledge, but also provides the rationale for performing the experiment. In other words, when the reader finishes reading this section, it should be clear to him that there is a void in the knowledge about the subject matter which creates a need for the present experiment.

IV. *Method* - In this section the actual methodology of the experiment is described. Included here are usually several subheadings as illustrated below:

Apparatus or Equipment - Under this subheading, the materials and or instrumentation of the experiment are described in some detail, including a description of the setting in which the experiment was conducted.

Subjects - If human or animal subjects are used as an actual part of the experiment, rather than just the manipulation of the physical properties of objects, a detailed description of the characteristics of the population must be provided. For example, "Twenty normal hearing subjects (Nine males and eleven females) Ranging in age from sixteen to forty-one years (mean age of twenty years) served as research subjects."

Procedure - This is a detailed accounting of exactly what transpired in the experiment: What variables were manipulated and how, what variables were held constant and how, what instructions did the subject receive, how was the data collected and transcribed, etc.

Analysis of Data - This is a simple statement of the methods used in analyzing the data produced by the experiment, including any statistical methods which were utilized.

V. *Results* - Included in this section are all of the derived data, means, figures, graphs, and other representational measures of the original raw data which are mathematically derived by some standard technique, such as means, medians- modes, etc. In the strict "APA style" all of the data are reported in this section, i.e., raw and derived. In speech pathology and audiology reports, the raw data is usually contained in an appendix, or in the case of published articles, can be obtained by request from the author.

VI. *Discussion* - This is the section of the report in which the experimenter is allowed to interpret the results. In other words, the results are interpreted in terms of whether or not the original posed question was adequately answered by the experiment or whether or not the originally posed hypothesis was accepted or rejected. Next, the experimenter is free to speculate about the implications of the results of the experiment as they relate to the status of knowledge on the subject matter. He may wish to speculate about the effects of the study on theory about a problem, or he may wish to discuss the implications for clinical practice or for future research in this particular area.

Invariably, a researcher discovers weakness in his experimental plan that he only becomes aware of during or after the experiment. It is in the discussion section that he openly discusses these weaknesses and how they may have affected the outcome of the study. Moreover, he usually suggests ways of repairing the weaknesses for those who want to duplicate the study or do studies which are similar.

VII. *Summary and Conclusions* - This is really a one-or two-paragraph statement that summarizes or offers a precis of all the sections listed in the formal report. It is this section along with the title of the research project which is read by potential readers, aiding them in making their determination about whether or not they would desire to read the entire project. The student will quickly learn this latter fact himself as he performs his review of the literature in preparation for his own research project.

RESEARCH PROPOSAL

Most experimental research done by students has as a prerequisite the submission and approval of a research proposal. This process allows the student to receive advice from those more experienced in such matters on the appropriateness of his research plan, the soundness of his judgment about what variables to manipulate, and the appropriateness of the proposed methods of analyzing the data, etc. If done properly, the research proposal is, in actuality, the first several sections of the research report. In other words, the research proposal is a statement of the problem, a review of the pertinent literature, the proposed method of performing the experiment, including the proposed list of apparatus, number and kind of subjects required, description of variable manipulation, proposed method of data analysis, and, usually, a predictive statement about the possible outcome of the experiment and possible implications of that outcome. It can be seen that a carefully planned and organized approved proposal serves very nearly the same function as the outline which evolved when organizing the non-experimental research report. In other words, once a research proposal has been approved, the student merely needs to follow the proposal precisely, keeping very careful notes and when the work is done he translates these notes into the final report form.

Presented below is another actual paper prepared by a student. This paper, however, represents a simple experimental research project. This paper, as the first, was not prepared with any intention of publication. It represents an exercise rather than a detailed, carefully controlled experiment. Again, we have taken liberties, with the student's permission, in order to illustrate common errors.

A COMPARISON OF PULSED AND CONTINUOUS PURE TONE AIR CONDUCTION THRESHOLDS USING CLINICAL AUDIOMETRIC TECHNIQUES

By

Lynn C. Brewster

Submitted in Partial Fulfillment
of the Requirements for
Introduction to Research

STATEMENT OF THE PROBLEM

This experiment was designed to answer two questions: Will the use of a pulsed pure tone stimulus result in a lower audiotry threshold than a continuous pure tone stimulus, and will there be a greater threshold differential between these two stimuli at higher frequencies? These two questions will be pursued using the clinical technique developed by Carhart and Jerger.

Hypothesis

Two hypotheses were explored. First, it was hypothesized that the thresholds for pulsed pure tone air conduction stimuli would be lower than the thresholds for continuous pure tone stimuli, and second, there would be a greater difference between pulsed pure tone thresholds and continuous pure tone thresholds at 2000 Hz than between pulsed pure tone thresholds and continuous pure tone thresholds at 250 Hz.

REVIEW OF THE LITERATURE

Hirsch pointed out that "a tone that does not change in either amplitude or frequency is more diffi-

[1]Raymond Carhart and James F. Jerger, Preferred Method for Clinical Determination of Pure-tone Thresholds," *Journal of Speech and Hearing Disorders*, XXIV (1959), 330-345.

[2]Ira J. Hirsh, *The Measurement of Hearing* (New York: McGraw-Hill, 1952), 113.

[3]*Ibid.*, pp. 101-102.

cult to listen to, to attend to, than a tone that is changed in at least one dimension." From the physiological point of view, neural responses are more easily elicited

The reader will note that the footnotes numbering begins with "1" on each page. This is acceptable. One may begin with "1" on each page, at the beginning of each chapter, or they may run in one series throughout the paper.

by changing stimuli than by continuous stimuli. [In this study, the stimuli was changed by presenting a pulsed tone of 0.5 seconds on and 0.5 seconds off. Information of this nature would lead one to believe that thresholds under pulsed pure tone conditions would be lower than thresholds under continuous pure tone conditions.]

This statement is misplaced; it belongs in the methods section.

The threshold change which should supposedly occur under pulsed pure tone conditions as opposed to continuous pure tone stimuli may depend upon other factors, such as auditory adaptation and recovery. Jerger defines auditory adaptation as the "result of rendering non-functional a certain proportion of neural elements which initially responded to the stimulus." Recovery

[1]Arnold M. Small. "Auditory Adaptation", in *Modern Developments in Audiology*, ed. by James F. Jerger (New York: Academic Press, 1963), 314.

The use of "then" implies that the preceding statement provided at least partial explanation. In this case, it did not. It would best be left out.

time, then, is the amount of time required for the nonfuctional proportion of neural elements to again become functional.

Essentially, there are three basic factors which affect the degree and rate of adaptation and recovery. These include: (1) frequency of the adapting stimulus, (2) loudness of the adapting stimulus and (3) duration of the adapting stimulus. Jerger stated that more adaptation occurred for the higher frequencies; however; it should be pointed out that he used an SPL reference level. He concluded that these results had little meaning unless the intensities of the adapting stimuli were converted into loudness levels and the frequencies of the adapting stimuli were converted into sones. From these transformed results, no significant differences were obtained, thus Jerger concluded that loudness had more of a direct effect than did frequency.[1] This would support the results of the present experiment in which no significant difference was found between the differences in threshold for pulsed and continuous pure tones at 250 Hz and 2000 Hz. [It should be pointed out that Jerger used a continuous pure tone stimulus; therefore, one cannot generalize to other stimuli.]

A familiar error. Jerger is the editor of the book in which Small writes of "Adaptation." Check the footnote.

This statement is misplaced; it belongs in the results

Hirsh reported that the difference between thresholds obtained utilizing

[1] *Ibid.*, p. 301.

continuous pure tone techniques was larger for higher frequencies than those obtained utilizing continuous pure tone techniques was larger for higher frequencies than those obtained utilizing non-continuous stimuli.[2]

With respect to the concepts of adaption and recovery, very little conclusive information is available. However, it would seem that some relationship does exist between loudness and the amount of adaption which occurs and the recovery period required for the auditory mechanism to return to its normal state. Bocca and Calearo state that most researchers are in agreement with the statement that ". . . the time taken to reach asymtote or steady-state increases as the intensity of the adapting stimulus increases (in intensity)."[1] This phenomenon seems to hold true for pulsed stimuli as well as continuous stimuli.[2] [In this study the concern lay with hearing thresholds, consequently, the intensity of the stimulus was small so the time required to reach asymtote was short. It is unlikely, however, that asymtote was reached in 0.5 seconds. Because of this short time and the lack of adequate methodologi-

This is another misplac statem This belongs in the discussi sectio

[2]Hirsh, *Measurements*, p. 102.

[1]E. Bocca and C. Calearo, "Central Hearing Processes," in *Modern Developments in Audiology*, ed. by James F. Jerger (New York: Academic Press, 1963), 338-340.

[2]*Ibid.*, p. 333.

cal techniques, it would be virtually impossible to tell at this point how much adaptation did occur during the one-half second "on" period.]

The misplacement of statements frequently appears in beginning experimental papers. The "reviews of literature" section is included strictly for the purpose of informing the reader about the current status of knowledge, and provides a rationale for performing the experiment.

Sergeant and Harris illustrated that the length of time required for recovery is equal to the adaptation rate.[3] This would support the assumption made in this study that the use of a 0.5 second on-time and a 0.5 second off-time would allow for sufficient recovery of the auditory mechanism. Once again, however, the literature is in disagreement. Jerger suggested that the recovery rate is longer in duration than the rate of adaptation; consequently, it is improbable to assume that adaptation was counteracted by the 0.5 recovery period.[1]

Rose has suggested that pure tone threshold tests be administered using pulsed pure tone testing techniques

There is a problem here. Can you find it?

[3]Russell L. Sergeant and J. Donald Harris, "The Relation of Perstimulatory Adaptation to Other Short-Term Threshold Shifting Mechanisms", *Journal of Speech and Hearing Research*, VI (1963), 302.

[1]Small, *"Adaptation"*, p. 318.

HINT: Rose is the editor

in clinical audiometry.[2] However, continuous pure tone threshold tests are the typically used clinical technique.

Petty, Fraser and Elliot state the significant neural auditory adaptation occurs in the first two seconds of tonal stimulation.[3] Since the majority of the conventional pure tone threshold audiometric tests conducted require the presentation of a continuous stimulus for a duration between one and two seconds, it would seem appropriate to consider the factor of adaptation on thresholds.[4] Pulsed presentation could decrease the effect if adaptation because of the short stimulus presentation time. [Small has stated that a greater degree of auditory adaptation occurs for higher frequencies than lower frequencies.[5]]

This stateme is not directly related the discussio which preceded it.

The student has presented a review of the literature and has pointed out two areas where she feels there is a gap in information. Questions which the student has posed are:

(1) Do auditory threshold testing procedures which use a continuous pure tone stimulus actually alter threshold and make it poorer than it is?

---

[2]Lloyd L. Price, "Pure-tone Audiometry", in *Audiological Assessment*, ed. by Darrell E. Rose (New York: Prentice-Hall, 1971), 189.

[3]John W. Petty, Ronald D. Fraser and Frank N. Elliot, "Adaptation and Loudness Decrement: A Reconsideration", *American Acoustical Society Journal*, XLVII (1970), 1975.

[4]Carhart and Jerger, *"Preferred Method"*, 333.

[5]Small, *"Adaptation"*, p. 329.

(2) Will the use of a pulsed tone avoid adaptation and thus provide more accurate threshold values?

(3) Is there greater auditory adaptation at the higher frequencies than the lower frequencies?

Based upon the review of literature and the questions raised the student developed her hypothesis.

METHOD

Apparatus

All testing was performed in an IAC 40CTL two room sound proofed booth using a Maico MA-24 diagnostic audiometer. All audiometric test equipment was calibrated to ISO 1964 specifications. Pulse rate for the pulsed pure tone air conduction threshold test was 0.5 seconds on and 0.5 seconds off.

Subjects

Twenty college students (10 males and 10 females) with a mean age of 20.1 and a range of 18.2 to 26.5 years participated in this study. Subjects were volunteers from the Minot State College Social Science Division. Only subjects whose thresholds for the continuous pure tone threshold test which were below 15dB were included in this study.

Procedure

All subjects were administered a

pulsed pure tone air conduction threshold test and a continuous pure tone air conduction threshold test. Thresholds for both conditions were found for frequencies of 250 Hz and 2000 Hz. Half of the females and half the males were presented the pulsed pure tone threshold test first and the other half were presented the continuous pure tone threshold test first. Male and female subjects were alternated for test administration.

The method of clinical audiometric testing proposed by Carhart and Jerger was employed using a five-decibel intensity interval. This interval was employed rather than a smaller interval because (under these conditions) finer discrimination would not be meaningful and audiometric testing procedures were less complicated.

The examiner was a graduate clinician and was not aware of the hypotheses of the experiment. She was merely given the technique to be used, the frequencies to be tested, the order of testing the various conditions and the degree of increment to be employed.

Analysis of Data

Student's t test for the difference between means was applied for statistical analysis.

Reference for student's t test should be provided.

[1]Carhart and Jerger", *"Preferred Method"*, pp. 334-338.

RESULTS

A direct differece "t" test was administered to determine whether or not a significant difference existed between hearing threshold levels under pulsed pure tone conditions for 250 Hz and 2000 Hz. The "t" was not significant at the .01 level or the .05 level.

A second direct difference "t" was administered to determine whether or not a significant difference existed between the hearing threshold levels under pulsed pure tone conditions and continuous pure tone conditions. The value of "t" was not significant at the .01 or the .05 level.

DISCUSSION

The results of this experiment indicate that the hypothesis of this study should be rejected. Thresholds for pulsed pure tone aid conduction stimuli were not lower than the thresholds for continuous pure tone aid conduction stimuli were not lower than the thresholds for continuous pure tone air conductions stimuli presented at 250 Hz and 2000 Hz. Further, a greater difference did not exist between the pulsed and continuous thresholds at 2000 Hz than the pulsed and continuous thresholds obtained at 250 Hz.

When interpreting these results, three factors should receive consideration: (1) the use of the five dB increment, (2) the length of time required for recovery from adaptation, and (3) the duration of the pulsed tone.

The use of the five dB increments in this study may have resulted in the lack of significant differences between pulsed pure tone conditions for both hypotheses. Hirsh pointed out that the difference between pulsed and continuous thresholds under free field conditions is usually between five and six dB.[1] Consequently, the use of a five dB increment may have been too large to detect the difference. The use of a smaller increment, however, raises the question of meaningful differences. The accuracy of one dB increments with untrained subjects is highly suspect.[2] For results using one dB increments to be meaningful, trained observers would almost be a necessity as well as an examiner with considerable experience in expermental psychoacoustics. The time factor involved in using trained subjects and the inaccessibility of such an examiner ruled out the use of the one dB increment.

[1]Hirsh, *Measurement*, p. 102.

[2]Aram Glorig, *Audiometry: Principles and Practices,* (Baltimore: Williams and Wilkins, 1965), p. 89.

One other factor influenced the use of the five dB increment. This study is basically concerned with the clinical aspect of determining hearing thresholds. Consequently, the use of the five dB increment, which is most frequently employed in clinical audiometry, is more realistic to consider.[3]

Jerger pointed out that if complete recovery does not occur during the time off of the pulsed tone, then adaptation occurring from the preceding pulse (which has not yet been accounted for by recovery) will be carried over to the next pulse. This phenomenon will continue until the amount of adaptation occurring during stimulation equals the amount of recovery which occurs during off time, as adaptation approaches asymtote, the amount of recovery will more closely approximate the amount of

The student has committed an error frequently committed by the beginning writer. Footnote two, page 90, provides the name of the editor. The information actually came from Wallace S. High who contributed a chapter, "Some Problems of Measurement and Methodology in Auditory Research," to the book edited by Glorig. Improper footnoting gives credit to the wrong source, and should be avoided! The problem is compounded by not listing High in the bibliography.

[3]Carhart and Jerger, *"Preferred Method"*, p. 335.

adaptation.[1]

It is quite possible that the one-half second off-time did not allow for the auditory mechanism from the preceding one-half second presentation. As a result, threshold differences were not significant, possibly because of the cumulative effect of adaptation as a result of insufficient recovery time.

It is extremely possible that the use of the 0.5 second on-time and the 0.5 second off-time may also have had some effect on the results of this experiment. This particular choice of duration of pulses was made on the basis of necessity rather than choice. This was the only pulse setting on the Maico-24 audiometer. Hirsh suggested that an inverse relationship exists between the duration and hearing threshold levels for bursts ranging in duration from 1/4 to 33 tones per second with equal off-time.[1] It would seem possible that 0.5 second duration was not short enough in duration to result in a difference in threshold which could be detected by the crude measures employed in this study.

It would seem obvious that this experiment has neglected to take many aspects of the psychoacoustical principles into consideration and as a result, this experiment is of little help in determining whether or not threshold differences do exist be-

---

[1]Small, *"Adaptation"*, p. 318.

tween pulsed and continuous pure tone stimuli. It does, however, suggest that using standard clinical procedures for testing pure tone hearing threshold levels is not improved by pulsed stimuli. In other words, the techniques employed in clinical testing are not fine enough to detect any difference which may result from using pulsed or continuous stimuli.

SUMMARY AND CONCLUSIONS

Hearing thresholds were established for twenty college students. Thresholds were obtained under pulsed pure tone conditions and continuous pure tone conditions for frequencies of 250 Hz and 200 Hz.

Two hypotheses were proposed: (1) thresholds for pulsed pure tone air conduction stimuli would be lower than the thresholds for continuous pure tone stimuli, (2) there would be a greater difference between pulsed pure tone thresholds at 250 Hz. Both of the hypotheses were rejected and it was concluded that the clinical audiometric technique proposed by Carhart and Jerger did not provide a delicate enough measuring device to detect any difference which might have been present.

[1]Hirsh, *Measurement*, p. 102.

BIBLIOGRAPHY

Carhart, Raymond and Jerger, James F.: Preferred Method for Clinical Determination of Pure-Tone Thresholds, Journal of Speech and Hearing Disorders, XXIV (1959), p. 330-345.

Hirsh, Ira J.: The Measurement of Hearing, (New York: McGraw-Hill, 1952), p. 101-113.

Jerger, James F.: Modern Developments in Audiology, (New York: Academic Press, 1963), p. 328-340.

Petty, John W. Fraser, Ronald D., and Elliot, Frank N.: Adaptation of Loudness Decrement: A Reconsideration, American Acoustical Society Journal, 45 (1957), 1063-1978.

Rose, Darrell E.: Audiological Assessment, (New York: Prentice-Hall, 1971), p. 189.

Sergeant, Russell L. and Harris, J. Donald: The Relation of Perstimulatory Adaptation to Other Short-Term Threshold Shifting Mechanisms, Journal of Speech and Hearing Research, VI (1963), p. 27-39.

CHAPTER IV

INFORMATIONAL SOURCES

We have already supplied selected lists of references; both survey sources and specific interest area sources (see Chapter II). In this chapter we will attempt to guide the student to other informational sources.

There are many sources of information. Listed below are some of the organizations, journals, reviews, and abstracts which provide information about speech pathology and audiology and/or speech, voice, language, and hearing disorders. It is not intended that any of these lists be either comprehensive or exhaustive. Again, they are designed to help the student get going.

ORGANIZATIONS

The American Speech and Hearing Association
9030 Old Georgetown Road
Washington, D.C.

In addition to publishing its own journals and periodicals, ASHA can provide information about the fields of Speech Pathology and Audiology such as: job opportunities, educational requirements, etc.

The Information Center for Hearing, Speech and Disorders of Human Communication

310 Harriet Lane Home, The John Hopkins Medical Institutions
Baltimore, Maryland 21205

The center prepares, publishes and distributes bibliographies in hearing, speech and disorders of communication. One may write to them to obtain a listing of available bibliographies.

The Volta Bureau
1537 35th Street Northwest
Washington, D.C. 20007

The Volta Bureau was founded by Alexander Graham Bell from funds received from his invention of the telephone. The Bureau provides information about the deaf and includes information in the area of Audiology.

The Easter Seal Society
2023 West Ogden Avenue
Chicago, Illinois 60612

While the Society provides services and information for a broad range of handicapping conditions, they do have material available in the area of Speech Pathology and Audiology. The available material consists essentially of reprints of articles from professional literature.

GENERAL REFERENCE WORKS

The following descriptions are intended to provide the student with a general impression of the publication and content. Familiarization by the student of the periodicals available in Speech Pathology and Audiology will save a great deal of time and effort. One can, by referring to the listing, determine which periodical is likely to appropriate for specific types of information.

A comment follows each review and publication description to indicate the general level of the material. The judgment of the level has been made solely by the authors of this text, and does not represent decisions made by editors of the journals or any professional organization.

Reviews

The *Annual Review of Psychology* reviews the perceptual processes of audition and psycholinguistics. The content will best be understood by the advanced undergraduate student. A bibliography is included.

Annual Review of Physiology - Periodically (each third or fourth year) a review of audition is presented. The discussions usually are appropos only to the advanced student in audiology.

Abstracts and Indexes

Biological Abstracts is published semimonthly in addition to a broad scope of topics which deal with sense organs, associated structures and functions are abstracted; thus, information related to the speech and hearing mechanisms are included.

Child Development Abstracts and Bibliography is published three times a year. Articles relative to audition, speech and language in child development are included.

Current Index to Journals in Education is a monthly publication that covers over 700 publications.

Educational Resources Information Center (ERIC) cummulates the indexes that appear in the monthly issues of *Research in Education.*

Research supported by HEW funds is abstracted.

Exceptional Child Education Abstracts is published four times a year. The primary focus of the abstract is the education of the handicapped with emphasis on teaching methods.

Research Relating to Children is published by Eric Clearinghouse on Early Childhood Education and placed for sale by the Superintendent of Documents, U.S. Government Property Office. The bulletin is published quarterly and contains a review of all abstracts of research dealing with children and includes speech, language and hearing.

Periodicals

Annals of Otology, Rhinology and Laryngology is a bi-monthly medical publication. There are articles frequently included which are of interest to the speech pathologist or audiologist. Many articles are not beyond the understanding of advanced undergraduate and graduate students.

Archives of Otolaryngology, while published principally for medical specialists in ear, nose and throat, does often contain information of interest to the audiologist. The journal is of value to the advanced undergraduate and graduate level students.

ASHA, a journal of the American Speech and Hearing Association, is published monthly. The journal contains information pertinent to association members. Each issue contains articles, special reports, news and announcements, countless reports and book reviews. The publication is valuable to students at all levels of training.

Audiology is published bi-monthly. The articles are essentially experimental and thus are best understood by the advanced graduate student.

British Journal of Audiology is published quarterly by the Royal National Institute for the Deaf. The journal presents a wide range of subject material in audiology, both of clinical and experimental nature. Many of the articles will be of value to undergraduate, and graduate students alike.

British Journal of Disorders of Communication, published quarterly, presents a variety of information pertinent to speech pathology and audiology. It is recommended for undergraduate and graduate students.

The Cleft Palate Journal publishes information relative to cleft lip and palate and problems associated with this birth defect. Advanced undergraduate and graduate level students will both benefit.

Folia Phoniatrica is an international journal which publishes articles related to experimental phonetics, speech disorders, and language disorders and also theoretical papers. It is recommended for graduate level students.

Hearing and Speech News is published montlhy by the National Association of Hearing and Speech Agencies. Articles are related to rehabilitation in speech and hearing. Suitable for undergraduate level students.

Journal of the Acoustical Society of America, a monthly publication, publishes papers on acoustics. There are frequently papers dealing with speech and audition that are valuable to the speech pathologist and aduiologist. The material is best suited to the graduate level student.

Journal of Auditory Research is an inter-disciple quarterly for "all workers seriously interested in the scientific study of hearing." The contents will probably best be understood by students at the graduate level.

Journal of Communication Disorders publishes articles on problems related to disorders of communication. Experimental reports, case studies and theoretical papers are included. The articles include both speech pathology and audiology with material which is of interest to the advanced undergraduate and graduate student.

Journal of Speech and Hearing Disorders is published by the American Speech and Hearing Association. The published articles cover clinical research, case studies, evaluation and remedial procedures in speech pathology and audiology. Students at all levels should be acquainted with this publication.

Journal of Speech and Hearing Research is published by the American Speech and Hearing Association. The papers presented are concerned with theoretical issues and research in speech pathology and audiology. Students at all levels should be acquainted with this publication.

Journal of Verbal Learning and Verbal Behavior is a bi-monthly publication. The publication will be of value to students with a special interest in language. Recommended for graduate level students.

Language, Speech and Hearing Services in the School is published by the American Speech and Hearing Association and is related to research, clinical procedures, program organization and management and professional responsibility. Students at all levels should be familiar with this publication.

Maico Audiological Library Series is an irregular serial published by Maico Electronics and covers a broad range of subjects related to clinical audiology. The series is recommended for advanced undergraduate and graduate students.

Quarterly Journal of Speech is directed primarily to speech communication. Prior to approximately 1950, numerous articles dealing with speech and hearing appeared. Since the 50's, however, only a few scattered papers related to speech pathology or audiology are published. The journal articles which appear before 1950 are of historical value and are recommended to students at all levels of training.

Rehabilitation Record is a bi-monthly publication dealing with rehabilitation of the handicapped. Included in the publication are papers related to rehabilitation of the speech and hearing handicapped. The level is suitable (even recommended) for undergraduate students.

APPENDIX A

REFERENCING PROCEDURES IN REPORT WRITING

Many students often show confusion when referencing a paper; this need not occur. Once the student understands the purpose of referencing, the acceptable procedures are easily used. Referencing requires the use of footnotes and a bibliography.

Footnotes serve to provide information to the reader regarding the authority for statements in the text, cross references, acknowledgment, and additional comments which amplify or qualify the textual discussion. There are, then, two general types of footnotes: reference and content. In recent years, most professional journals have moved from referencing in footnotes to referencing within the body of the text. The reader must keep in mind that the type of reporting for term papers, thesis and dissertations may differ somewhat from the style required to prepare a manuscript for publication. When preparing for publication, the style required by the specific journal must be used. There is, however, one very important aspect of referencing: consistency. If you begin your paper with a particular referencing style, use it throughout the paper. The following fictitious references will provide examples of methods:

> . . . and will experience dysfluency ninety percent of the time (4).

> . . . and will experience dysfluency ninety percent of the time (Squibble, 1973).

> . . . and will experience dysfluency ninety percent of the time.[1]

For the first example given, the reader turns to the fourth entry of the bibliography for the complete reference. To find the complete reference for example two, the reader again turns to the bibliography and finds Paul R. Squibble in the alphabetical listing for the complete reference. The third example provides the reference in a footnote which is readily available to the reader. All, however, are acceptable referencing methods.

BIBLIOGRAPHY

The bibliography lists the sources used within the text of the report. The general rules of preparing entries are common to most style and publication manuals. The specific examples are consistent with Kate L. Turabian's *A Manual for Writers of Term Papers, Thesis, and Dissertations*, 3rd Edition, Revised (Chicago: The University of Chicago Press, 1967).

GENERAL RULES

Book entries should include:

1. Full name of author(s), editors, or institutions responsible

2. Full title, including subtitle if one exists
3. Series, if any
4. Volume number
5. Editions, if not the original
6. City, publisher, and ate of publication

Article entries should include:

1. Name of author
2. Title or article
3. Name of Periodical
4. Volume number, date, or both
5. Pates

The information for authors in the publications of the American Speech and Hearing Association specify that referencing within the text should be cited by author's surname and year of publication rather than by reference number. For example:

> . . . and will experience dysfluency ninety perdent of the time (Squibble, 1973).

> . . . as showed by Squibble (1973) will experience dysfluency ninety percent of the time.

The bibliography lists the sources used in the writing of the paper. To assist the student, specific examples likely to be frequently encountered in Speech Pathology and Audiology are provided.

[1]Paul R. Squibble: Stuttering Behavior Under Emotional Stress, *Journal of Strange Things*, XXVI (Nov., 1973), 111.

Specific Examples

Book With One Author

Whitfield, I.C.: *The Auditory Pathway.* Baltimore: The Williams & Wilkins Co., 1967.

Book With Two Authors

Berry, Mildred F., and Eisenson, J.N.: *Speech Disorders*: Principles *and Practices of Thearapy.* New York: Applteton-Century-Crofts, Inc., 1956.

Book With Three Authors

Schuvell, Mildred, Jenkins, James J. and Jiminez-Pabon, Edward: *Aphasia in Adults.* New York: Harper & Row, 1964.

Book With More Than Three Authors

Johnson, Wendell, *et al.: Speech Handicapped School Children.* Revised Edition. New York: Harper & Bros., 1956.

Book With An Association As Author

Association for Research in Nervous and Mental Disease: Disorders of Communication, Proceedings of the Association. Baltimore: Williams & Wilkins, 1964.

Book By Editor(s)

Wingo, John W. and Holloway, Gordon F., eds.: *An Appraisal of Speech Pathology and Audiology: A Symposium.* Springfield, Illinois: Charles C Thomas. 1973.

Translation Book In Which Author Is Known

Portman, Michael and Portland, Claudine: *Clincial Audiometry,* translated by Bruce Proctor and Sheila Weaver. Springfield, Illinois: Charles C Thomas. 1961

Paper back Edition Of A Book, first published in hard cover

Denes, Peter B. and Pinson, Elliot N.: *The Speech Chain*, Anchor Science Study Series, Graden Center, New York: Anchor Books, 1973.

Periodical

Richards, Alan M.: Loudness Growth Under Masking: Relation to True Sensorineural Impairment, *Journal of Speech and Hearing Research*, XVI (December, 1973), 597-607.

Paper Read Or Speech Delivered At Meeting

Holloway, Gordon F.: The Teaching of Clinical Methodology. Paper read at the Annual Convention, American Speech and Hearing Association, November 5, 1972, Chicago, Illinois.

Thesis on Dissertation

Webster, L. Michael: "A Cinematic Analysis of the Effects of Contingent Stimulation on Stuttering and Associated Behavior." Unpublished Ph.D. Dissertation, Southern Illinois University, 1965.

Documents

Citing documents is always a difficult problem because their forms vary so much. The form used should be one that makes them readily accessible to anyone wishing to locate them in the library. The library card catalogue will serve as a guide and the following general rules may help.

1. Identify the country, state, city, or other government district.
2. Identify the branch of government.
3. Identify the sub-branch(es). The sub-branch will likely be the "author" of the document.
4. The title of the document follows the "author."

www.ingramcontent.com/pod-product-compliance
Lightning Source LLC
LaVergne TN
LVHW010841051026
849532LV00007B/2782

دوست رہنما فلسفی

(مزاحیہ مضامین)

کنہیالال کپور

Dost Rahnuma Falsafi *(Humorous Essays)*
by: Kanhaiya Lal Kapoor
Edition: December '2025
Publisher :
Taemeer Publications LLC (Michigan, USA / Hyderabad, India)

ISBN 978-93-6908-755-6

9 789369 087556

کتاب	:	**دوست رہنما فلسفی** (مزاحیہ مضامین)
مصنف	:	**کنہیالال کپور**
صنف	:	طنز و مزاح
ناشر	:	تعمیر پبلی کیشنز (حیدرآباد، انڈیا)
سالِ اشاعت	:	۲۰۲۵ء
صفحات	:	۹۲
سرورق ڈیزائن	:	تعمیر ویب ڈیزائن

فہرست

دیوانہ گر نہیں ہے تو...

یک لخت وہ محفل میں وارد ہوئے اور سب کے چہروں پر ہوائیاں اڑنے لگیں۔ جو ذرا زیادہ کم ہمت تھے دل ہی دل میں جل تو جلال تو کا وظیفہ پڑھنے لگے۔ وجہ یہ کہ نووارد محمد تغلق کے خاندان سے تعلق رکھتے ہیں اس لئے ہمیشہ یہ ڈر رہتا ہے کہ خدا جانے وہ کس وقت کس سے کیا کہہ دیں۔ کرسی پر دراز ہونے کے بعد انھوں نے اہلِ محفل کی طرف معنی خیز نظروں سے دیکھا اور فرمایا۔

"یہ آج کلب میں غیر معمولی سناٹا کیوں ہے۔ کوئی بات کیجئے"۔

کسی نے ڈرتے ڈرتے کہا۔ "تھک گئے ہیں"۔

"واہ۔ تھکاوٹ کی بھی ایک ہی کہی۔ تھک گئے ہیں تو شیش آسن کیجئے۔ تھکاوٹ دور کرنے کا بہترین طریقہ ہے"۔

اور وہ سر کے بل کھڑے ہو کر شیش آسن کا مظاہرہ کرنے لگے۔ جب

جی بھر کر مظاہرہ کر چکے تو کہا "تندرستی کے لئے دو چیزیں اشد ضروری ہیں۔ شیش آسن اور ایسب غول"

کلب کے کسی ممبر نے محض چھیڑنے کے لئے کہا "اس دن تو آپ فرما رہے تھے کہ صحت کو برقرار رکھنے کے لئے ہر روز ایک آنولہ کھانا چاہیئے۔"

"آنولہ بھی اچھی چیز ہے۔ لیکن اسیب غول کا مقابلہ نہیں کر سکتا"

"دودھ کے متعلق کیا ارشاد ہے۔"

"دودھ کو تو میں زہر سمجھتا ہوں۔ دودھ اسی فی صد بیماریوں کا ذمہ دار ہے۔ چاہے وہ ماں کا ہو یا بکری کا"

"بھینس کا دودھ تو شاید اتنا خراب نہیں ہوتا"

"بھینس کے دودھ سے بدتر شاید ہی کوئی چیز ہوگی۔ بھینس کا دودھ پینے والے کی عقل بھینس سے بھی موٹی ہو جاتی ہے۔ اس کی بجائے لیموں کا رس پینا چاہیئے اس میں وٹامن سی ہوتا ہے"

"سنا ہے وٹامن سی تو گھاس میں بھی ہوتا ہے"

"آپ ٹھیک کہتے ہیں لیکن سبز گھاس میں۔ خشک میں نہیں۔ خشک گھاس میں البتہ وٹامن ڈی ہوتا ہے"

"آپ سبز گھاس کھاتے ہیں یا خشک"

اس پر ایک زوردار قہقہہ لگا اور مجلس برخاست ہوگئی۔

کلب سے اٹھ کر گھر آئے۔ ابھی اخبار پڑھنے کے لئے اٹھایا ہی تھا کہ ایک اور صاحب تشریف لائے۔

"برا نہ مانیے گا!" انھوں نے بڑی نرمی سے کہا۔ "میں آپ کے پاس ایک شکایت لے کر آیا ہوں۔"

"کہیے۔"

"آپ کے بچے بہت شور مچاتے ہیں۔ میں مطالعہ نہیں کر سکتا۔ مطالعہ کے بغیر ریسرچ نہیں ہو سکتی۔ اور ریسرچ کے بغیر پی ایچ ڈی نہیں مل سکتی۔"

"میں بچوں سے کہہ دوں گا کہ وہ شور نہ مچایا کریں۔"

"نہیں نہیں میرا یہ مطلب نہیں۔ شور وہ بیشک مچایا کریں۔ لیکن جس وقت میں غسلخانے میں ہوتا ہوں اس وقت خاموش رہا کریں۔ بات یہ ہے کہ میں سوچنے کا کام غسلخانے میں کرتا ہوں۔ کچھ لوگ غسلخانے میں گانے لگتے ہیں یہ اوّل درجے کی بد مذاقی ہے۔ یہ تو ایسا ہی ہے جیسے کوئی ڈرام میں ناچنے لگے۔"

"آپ ریسرچ کس موضوع پر کر رہے ہیں؟"

"قطب مینار پر۔ میرا خیال ہے کہ قطب مینار کی گیارہ منزلیں تھیں سات نہیں۔ اب سوال یہ پیدا ہوتا ہے کہ وہ چار منزلیں کہاں گئیں۔"

"غالباً وہ کوئی بیرونی حملہ آور اپنے ساتھ لے گیا۔"

"میرا بھی یہی خیال ہے۔ لیکن سوال پھر پیدا ہوتا ہے کہ وہ حملہ آور کون تھا۔ ہندوستان میں کب آیا اور وہ صرف چار منزلیں اپنے ساتھ کیوں لے گیا۔ یعنی اس نے سالم قطب مینار کو اٹھانا کیوں مناسب نہ سمجھا؟"

"ممکن ہے وہ کسی حادثے کا شکار ہوگئی ہوں"

"ہوسکتا ہے۔ لیکن اب سوال تیسری بار پیدا ہوتا ہے کہ کون سے حادثے کی۔ بھونچال۔ سیلاب۔ ٹڈی دل۔ میرا مطلب ہے حادثے بھی تو کئی ہوسکتے ہیں"

"بہرحال موضوع بہت دلچسپ ہے۔ ریسرچ جاری رکھیے گا"

"ریسرچ تو جاری رکھوں گا ہی۔ لیکن آپ ذرا بچوں سے کہہ دیجئے کہ جب میں غسلخانے ۔ ۔ ۔ ۔"

"ہاں ہاں۔ وہ میں کہہ دوں گا"

صبح دفتر میں گئے ابھی بیٹھے ہی تھے کہ چپڑاسی نے اطلاع دی کہ بڑے صاحب یاد فرما رہے ہیں۔ بڑے صاحب کی خدمت میں حاضر ہوئے۔ انھوں نے اشارے سے کرسی پر بیٹھنے کے لئے کہا۔

"مسٹر رشید" انھوں نے فرمایا "میں نے آپ کو ایک نہایت ضروری کام سے بلایا ہے"

"ارشاد"

"وہ ضروری کام یہ۔۔۔۔ ہے۔۔۔ یہ تھا۔۔ کہ۔۔ ہاں۔۔ وہ کہ۔۔۔ کیا تھا وہ ضروری کام۔۔۔۔ اچھا آپ جا سکتے ہیں"

پندرہ بیس منٹ کے بعد انھوں نے پھر بلا بھیجا۔ "ہاں مسٹر رشید وہ ضروری کام یاد آگیا۔ کل ہفتے کا کون سا دن تھا؟"

"جی اتوار"

"اچھا آپ جا سکتے ہیں۔"

آدھ پون گھنٹے کے بعد انھوں نے پھر یاد فرمایا۔ "مسٹر رشید مجھے پتہ چلا ہے کہ آپ آفس میں سگرٹ پیتے ہیں۔ کیا یہ درست ہے؟"

"جی ہاں۔"

"دیکھیے آفس میں سگرٹ مت پیا کیجیے۔ اگر کسی فائل کو آگ لگ گئی، تو کون ذمہ دار ہوگا؟"

"آئندہ نہیں پیا کروں گا۔"

"اور ہاں۔ یہ سبز رنگ کی ٹائی پہن کر مت آیا کیجیے۔ مجھے سبز رنگ سے سخت نفرت ہے۔"

"بہت اچھا جناب۔"

"یہ آج آپ کی آنکھیں لال کیوں ہو رہی ہیں۔"

"غالباً اس لیے کہ رات گئے تک دفتر کا کام کرتا رہا۔"

"نہیں یہ وجہ نہیں ہو سکتی۔ آپ کا جگر خراب ہے۔ آپ گرم پانی کے گلاس روزانہ پیتے ہیں"

"گرم پانی تو نہیں البتہ چائے دو تین بار پیتا ہوں۔"

"چائے جگر کی نمبر ون دشمن ہے۔ چائے بالکل ترک کر دیجیے۔ گرم پانی کے گلاس پیا کیجیے۔"

"بہت اچھا جناب"

تین بجے کے قریب انھوں نے پھر بلا بھیجا۔ "مسٹر رشید۔ ابھی ابھی اطلاع

آئی ہے کہ انسپکٹر صاحب کل یہاں تشریف لائے ہیں۔ میں چاہتا ہوں کہ ان کے اعزاز میں ایک پارٹی کی جائے اور آپ اور دفتر کے باقی ملازم پارٹی پر ایک قوالی گائیں۔"

"لیکن بندہ پرور قوالی ہم کیسے گائیں گے۔ میرا مطلب ہے، کہ ہم میں سے کوئی..."

"گانا نہیں جانتا۔ یہی مطلب ہے نا آپ کا؟"

"جی ہاں۔"

"اس سے کیا فرق پڑتا ہے۔ آپ سیکھ سکتے ہیں؟"

"لیکن جناب ہم نے آج تک قوالی . . . ."

"میں کوئی عذر سننے کے لئے تیار نہیں۔ قوالی آپ کو گانا ہو گی۔ یہ میرا حکم ہے۔ آپ ابھی سے اس کی تیاری کیجئے۔"

"لیکن جناب دیکھئے نا۔ ہم قوالی . . . ."

"بحث کرنے کی ضرورت نہیں۔ آرڈر آرڈر ہے۔"

اپنا سا منہ لیکر دفتر سے باہر چلے آئے۔ تھکے ماندے گھر پہنچے۔ گراموفون پر کلھن قوال کی گائی ہوئی مشہور قوالی کا ریکارڈ لگایا۔ اور بیوی بچوں کے ساتھ تالیاں بجا بجا کر گانے لگے۔

دیکھا ہے ہم نے جلوت وخلوت میں اسد کو
دیوانہ گر نہیں ہے تو ہشیار بھی نہیں

مشاغل

کردار:

تک بند
مس فراون
مرزا خدشہ
میاں شکی
حلیم

مقام: ویٹنگ روم

تک بند: خواتین و حضرات! یہ تو ظاہر ہے کہ صبح سے پہلے گاڑی نہیں مل سکتی اور

وڈیننگ روم میں اتنے مچھر ہیں کہ دم بھر چین نہیں لینے دیتے۔ سونے کا سوال ہی نہیں پیدا ہوتا۔ مناسب معلوم ہوتا ہے کہ چپ چاپ بیٹھنے یا اونگھنے کی بجائے ایک دوسرے سے تعارف حاصل کیا جائے تاکہ وقت بھی کٹ جائے اور طبیعت بھی بشاش رہے۔

مس فراڈن: تجویز تو معقول ہے۔ تو آپ ہی بسم اللہ کیجئے نا۔

تک بند: خاکسار کو تک بند کہتے ہیں۔ واضح رہے کہ یہ میرا نام ہے تخلص نہیں۔

مس فراڈن: حالانکہ تخلص بھی ہوتا۔ تو کوئی مضائقہ نہیں تھا۔

تک بند: بجا فرماتی ہیں آپ۔ لیکن اگر تخلص ہوتا تو پھر مجھے تک بندی کی بجائے شاعری کرنا پڑتی۔ اس لئے خدا کا شکر ہے کہ یہ تخلص نہیں۔

مس فراڈن: آپ کا شغل؟

تک بند: شغل نام سے ہی ظاہر ہے۔ یعنی تک سے تک جوڑنا۔ دوسرے لفظوں میں قافیہ بندی۔ رات کا قافیہ برسات اور برسات کا قافیہ ملاقات سے ملاتا ہوں۔ حسن یار کا قافیہ نرگس بیمار۔ اور موخر الذکر کا قافیہ مصر کے بازار سے جوڑتا ہوں۔ واللہ وہ لطف آتا ہے کہ بیان نہیں کر سکتا۔

مس فراڈن: سبحان اللہ۔ آپ تو اچھے خاصے شاعر ہیں۔ حالانکہ تک بند آپ کا نام ہے تخلص نہیں۔

تک بند: جی نہیں میں شاعر نہیں ہوں۔ شعر کہنے کے لئے بڑا پتا مارنا پڑتا ہے۔ اور میرا پتا ذرا کمزور ہے۔

مس فراڈن: تو آپ نثر کیوں نہیں لکھتے۔ آخر تک بندی میں کیا دھرا ہے۔

تک بند: اچھی نثر لکھنا بھی کون سا آسان کام ہے۔ بڑے بڑوں کو خیر دعافیت معلوم ہو جاتی ہے۔

مس فراؤن: لیکن سوال یہ ہے کہ تک بندی کا فائدہ!

تک بند: فائدہ یہ کہ جس مجلس میں کلام پڑھتا ہوں، اس میں بھگدڑ مچ جاتی ہے۔ سامعین خدا کا شکر بجا لاتے ہیں کہ مشاعرہ ختم ہوا۔

مس فراؤن: پھر تو آپ بڑے کام کے آدمی ہیں۔

تک بند: آپ کی عنایت ہے۔ اچھا اب آپ اپنے متعلق کچھ فرمائیے۔

مس فراؤن: میرا نام مس فراؤن ہے۔

تک بند: بہت خوبصورت نام ہے۔ میری بھانجی کی بلی کا نام بھی فراؤن ہے۔

مس فراؤن: ہوگا۔ کچھ لوگ بلیوں کا نام رکھنے میں کافی حماقت کا ثبوت دیتے ہیں۔

تک بند: آپ کا شغل؟

مس فراؤن: شغل ذرا عجیب سا ہے۔ یعنی

تک بند: یعنی؟

مس فراؤن: ناک بھوں چڑھانا۔

تک بند: عجیب شغل ہے۔ ذرا اس کی وضاحت فرما دیجیے۔

مس فراؤن: میں ہر شخص اور ہر چیز کو دیکھ کر ناک بھوں چڑھاتی ہوں۔ مثال کے طور پر ان عورتوں پر جو سگرٹ نہیں پیتیں۔ ان بچوں پر جو لپٹے چپاکو نکل نہیں کہتے۔ ان خواتین پر جن کی گود میں پلے کی بجائے اپنا بچہ ہو تلمی۔

تک بند: معلوم ہوتا ہے آپ کی ناک بہت حساس واقع ہوئی ہے۔

مس فراؤن : افسوسناک حد تک حساس۔ دراصل مجھے ہر اُس چیز سے بُو آنے لگتی ہے جس پر مغرب کی مہر نہ ہو۔

تک بند: پھر تو آپ کو سورج پر بھی اعتراض ہوگا۔ کیونکہ یہ ہمیشہ مشرق سے طلوع ہوتا ہے۔

مس فراؤن: مجھے سورج بالکل پسند نہیں۔

تک بند: مشرقی علوم و فنون بھی آپ کو ناپسند ہوں گے۔

مس فراؤن: بالکل ناپسند۔

تک بند: کالی داس۔ اجنتا اور تاج محل کے متعلق آپ کا کیا خیال ہے؟

مس فراؤن: مجھے تو ان میں کوئی خاص بات نظر نہیں آتی۔

تک بند: آپ ایک دن میں اوسطاً کتنی بار ناک بھوں چڑھاتی ہیں۔

مس فراؤن: سیکڑوں بار۔

تک بند: کافی تھک جاتی ہوں گی۔

مس فراؤن: کئی بار تو اتنا تھک جاتی ہوں کہ اپنے پر ناک بھوں چڑھانے کو جی چاہتا ہے۔

تک بند: اگر آپ دوسروں کی بجائے صرف اپنے پر ناک بھوں چڑھائیں تو زیادہ اچھا ہے۔

مس فراؤن: آپ تو مذاق کرنے لگے..... اچھا اب ذرا ان کی باتیں بھی سُنیں۔ (تیسرے مسافر سے) آپ کی تعریف؟

مرزا خدشہ: ناچیز کو مرزا خدشہ کہتے ہیں۔

مس فراؤن : اف کتنا خطرناک نام ہے۔

مرزا خدشہ : گھبرائیے نہیں۔ میں کافی شریف آدمی ہوں۔

تک بند : کیا آپ کا شغل دریافت کر سکتا ہوں۔

مرزا خدشہ : شغل خاصہ بے ضرر ہے یعنی خطرے کی گھنٹی بجانا۔

مس فراؤن : کون سے خطرے کی؟

مرزا خدشہ : ہر قسم کے خطرے کی۔۔۔۔ آپ شاید نہیں جانتے کہ ہم بڑی خطرناک دنیا میں رہ رہے ہیں۔ یہاں قدم قدم پر خطرہ ہے۔ آپ نے شاید چند دن ہوئے آسمان پر ایک دُم دار ستارا دیکھا ہوگا۔

مس فراؤن : ہاں ہاں دیکھا تھا۔

مرزا خدشہ : نہایت خطرناک شگون ہے۔

مس فراؤن : وہ کیسے؟

مرزا خدشہ : یہ اس بات کی علامت ہے کہ قیامت آنیوالی ہے۔

مس فراؤن : آپ کو کیسے پتہ چلا کہ قیامت آرہی ہے۔

مرزا خدشہ : دُم دار ستارا جو طلوع ہوا ہے۔

تک بند : اس سے پہلے بھی آپ نے کبھی خطرے کی گھنٹی بجائی۔

مرزا خدشہ : کئی بار۔ تین ماہ ہوئے۔ ہم نے کہا تھا کہ تیسری عالمگیر جنگ شروع ہونیوالی ہے۔

تک بند : لیکن وہ شروع نہیں ہوئی۔

مرزا خدشہ : تھوڑی ہی کسر رہ گئی۔ ورنہ شروع ہو ہی گئی تھی۔

مس فراڈن : اس کے علاوہ بھی کوئی پیشین گوئی کی ؟

مرزا خدشہ : ڈیڑھ ماہ ہوا۔ ہم نے کہا تھا کہ قحط پڑنے والا ہے۔

مس فراڈن : لیکن یہ پیشین گوئی بھی غلط ثابت ہوئی۔

مرزا خدشہ : اس سے کیا فرق پڑتا ہے۔ اگر حالات ذرا بدتر ہو جاتے تو قحط پڑ سکتا تھا۔

تک بند : آپ کا طرزِ استدلال لاجواب ہے۔ اچھا یہ فرمائیے کہ یہ خطرے کی گھنٹی جسے آپ اکثر بجاتے رہتے ہیں آپ نے کہاں رکھی ہوئی ہے۔

مرزا خدشہ : رکھنا کہاں تھی قبلہ۔ وہ تو ہمارے دماغ میں ہے۔ جی ہاں دماغ میں۔

مس فراڈن : معلوم ہوتا ہے یہ سب قصور آپ کے دماغ کا ہے۔

تک بند : مرزا صاحب کیا آپ زحمت فرما کر بتا سکتے ہیں کہ اس ویٹنگ روم کی چھت تو گرنے والی نہیں۔

مرزا خدشہ : کوئی بھی چھت کسی وقت بھی گر سکتی ہے۔ دراصل آپ کسی چھت کے متعلق وثوق سے نہیں کہہ سکتے کہ وہ کب تک کھڑی رہے گی اور کب گر پڑے گی۔

تک بند : (چوتھے مسافر سے) آپ کچھ فرمائیے۔

میاں شکی : نام ہے میاں شکی اور شغل ہے شک کرنا۔

مرزا خدشہ : کافی دلچسپ شغل ہے۔ تو آپ ہر وقت شک کرتے رہتے ہیں۔

میاں شکی : بجا فرمایا آپ نے۔ میں ان لوگوں میں سے ہوں جنھیں اپنے سوا کوئی شخص قابلِ اعتبار نظر نہیں آتا۔ نوکر پر شک کرتا ہوں کہ کہیں میری غیر حاضری میں گھر کا سامان اٹھا کر رفو چکر نہ ہو جائے۔ باورچی پر شک

کرتا ہوں کہ کہیں کھانے میں زہر نہ ملا دے۔ گلی میں سے گذرتے ہوئے کتوں پر شک کرتا ہوں کہ کہیں مجھے کاٹ نہ کھائیں۔

مس فراؤن: لیکن سوال یہ ہے کہ آپ ایسا کیوں کرتے ہیں

میاں شکی: میں ضرورت سے زیادہ محتاط اور دانشمند واقع ہوا ہوں۔

تک بند: لیکن ہر شخص پر شک کرنا کہاں کی دانشمندی ہے۔

میاں شکی: دانشمندی کیوں نہیں۔ دیکھئے جس ہم سفر کو آپ شریف آدمی سمجھ رہے ہیں ممکن ہے وہ جیب کترا ہو۔ جس ہمسائے کو آپ پارسا سمجھتے ہیں ممکن ہے اس کی آنکھ آپ کی بیوی پر ہو۔ جس شخص کو آپ دوست تصور کرتے ہیں۔ ہو سکتا ہے وہ پہلے درجے کا دغا باز ہو۔

مس فراؤن: آپ کا اپنے متعلق کیا خیال ہے؟

میاں شکی: میں اپنے پر بھی اکثر شک کرتا ہوں۔ بسا اوقات مجھے شک گذرتا ہے کہ میرا دماغی توازن ٹھیک نہیں۔

مس فراؤن: اس وقت تو آپ کی حالت نہایت قابلِ رحم ہوتی ہوگی۔

میاں شکی: اس میں کیا شک ہے۔

مس فراؤن: (پانچویں مسافر سے) اچھا صاحب۔ آپ کافی عرصہ سے خاموش بیٹھے ہیں۔ آپ بھی کچھ فرمائیے۔

حلیم: میرا نام حلیم ہے۔

تک بند: حلیم! بڑا فضول سا نام ہے۔ سوائے رحیم اور کریم کے کوئی قافیہ ہی نہیں۔

مس فراؤن : آپ کا شغل ؟
حلیم : معلم ہوں ۔ لڑکوں کو پڑھاتا ہوں ۔ بیوی بچوں کا پیٹ پالتا ہوں۔
مس فراؤن : یہ تو آپ کا پیشہ ہوا شغل بتائیے ۔
حلیم : بس اسی کو شغل سمجھ لیجئے ۔
مس فراؤن : (چہک کر) اسے آپ شغل کہتے ہیں !
حلیم : یہ شغل نہیں تو اور کیا ہے ؟
تک بند : یہ شغل نہیں۔ محض تضیع اوقات ہے ۔
حلیم : معاف کیجئے ۔ مجھے آپ سے اتفاق نہیں ۔
مس فراؤن : اے بھئی ذرا ان کے ذہن کی داد دیجئے۔ ان کے خیال میں لڑکوں کو پڑھانا اور بیوی بچوں کا پیٹ پالنا بھی شغل ہے۔
مرزا خدشہ : (قہقہہ لگا کر) ہاہاہا۔ میاں عقل کے ناخن لو۔ لڑکوں کو پڑھانا اور بیوی بچوں کا پیٹ پالنا بھی کوئی شغل ہے ۔ ہاہاہا۔ ہاہاہا۔ بھئی حد ہوگئی۔

بات تو سُنئے

آپ پوچھتے ہیں کہ میں گھر سے باہر کیوں نہیں نکلتا۔ گوشہ نشینی کیوں اختیار کرلی ہے۔ کیا گھر میں بیٹھے بیٹھے میری طبیعت نہیں اوبتی! کیا میری صحت خراب نہیں ہوجائے گی؟ آپ بجا فرماتے ہیں۔ لیکن آپ خود ہی کہیئے کہ میں گھر سے کیسے نکل سکتا ہوں۔ بدقسمتی سے ایسے محلے میں رہتا ہوں جہاں سب ریٹائرڈ لوگ رہائش پذیر ہیں۔ یوں تو قریب ہر پڑھا لکھا شخص باتونی ہوتا ہے لیکن ریٹائرڈ لوگ تو گویا پیشہ ور باتونی ہوتے ہیں۔ لیجئے میں ابھی گھر سے نکلا ہوں کہ صوبیدار صاحب نے پکار کر کہا۔ "اجی پروفیسر صاحب کہاں چلدئے۔ بات تو سنئے۔ آئیے آپ کا تعارف اپنے نئے کتے سے کرائیں؟ جی ذرا ڈاک خانے تک چلا ہوں۔ ایک ضروری خط ڈالنا ہے۔" میں بڑی عاجزی سے کہتا ہوں — صوبیدار صاحب گرج کر فرماتے ہیں۔" اجی چھوڑیئے۔ خط آج کی ڈاک سے

نہیں جائے گا تو کونسی قیامت آجائے گی۔ مجھے دیکھئے تین مہینے خط کا جواب لکھنے میں صرف کرتا ہوں اور تین مہینے خط ڈالنے میں۔ ادھر آئیے آپ کو ایک چیز دکھائیں "۔ اور وہ چیز ہے ان کا ال سیشن کتا۔ ایسا خونخوار کتا دیکھ کر میرا تو خون خشک ہو رہا ہے کہ اگر کمبخت نے حملہ کر دیا تو۔ لیکن صوبیدار صاحب ہیں کہ کتے کی تعریف میں قصیدے پر قصیدہ پڑھ رہے ہیں۔

" جناب کتے تو ہم نے کئی پالے۔ لیکن کیا بات ہے اس ال سیشن کی، اتنا ذہین اتنا فرمانبردار، اتنا دلچسپ کہ کئی دفعہ شک ہونے لگتا ہے کہ یہ کتا ہے کہ معجزہ! آپ نے میرا دہ کتا دیکھا تھا جس کا نام تھا پسٹل۔ اور وہ بھی دیکھا ہو گا جسے میں اٹیم کے نام سے پکارا کرتا تھا۔ لیکن بخدا پروفیسر صاحب پسٹل اور اٹیم اس کتے کی گرد کو نہیں پہنچ سکتے۔ اس کی ہر بات ہی الگ ہے۔ بھونکنے کو ہی لیجیے۔ ویسے تو بھونکنا ہر کتے کی عادت ہی ہے۔ لیکن جناب جب یہ بھونکتا ہے تو معلوم ہوتا ہے۔ بھونک نہیں رہا۔ شعر پڑھ رہا ہے۔ شعر نہیں پڑھ رہا ہے۔ درباری کا الاپ کر رہا ہے کبھی سنئے اسے بھونکتے ہوئے۔ ایک اور وصف جو اس میں ہے۔ وہ یہ . . . . " قطع کلام معاف " میں ان کی بات کاٹ کر کہتا ہوں۔ " میں پھر کبھی حاضر ہوں گا۔ ڈاک کا وقت ہو رہا ہے "

مشکل سے پندرہ بیس گز کا فاصلہ طے کرتا ہوں کہ ماسٹر رنگی رام چلا کر کہتے ہیں۔ " پروفیسر صاحب میں نے کہا پروفیسر صاحب۔ ایک منٹ صرف ایک منٹ " ماسٹر رنگی رام کو معمے حل کرنے کا جنون ہے۔ اس لئے جب بھی ملتے ہیں معموں کی بات کرتے ہیں۔ " اچھا پروفیسر صاحب۔ اشارہ ہے کہ اگر یہ نہ

ہو تو زندگی کا مزا نہیں آتا۔ ممکن الفاظ ہیں بیوی اور بجلی۔ اچھا آپ کے خیال میں کون سا لفظ ٹھیک رہے گا؟" "جی میرے خیال میں تو بجلی موزوں جواب ہے۔" "کیسے؟"

"اس طرح کہ بیوی کے گھر آتے ہی زندگی کا سارا مزہ جاتا رہتا ہے"

"یہ تو عجیب منطق ہے۔ اچھا خیر۔ اپنا اپنا خیال ہے۔" ہاں دوسرا اشارہ ہے کہ اگر چل جائے تو بہت خوشی ہوتی ہے ممکن الفاظ ہیں۔" کھوٹی اٹھنی۔ کھوٹی چونی۔"

"میرے خیال میں کھوٹی اٹھنی ٹھیک ہے۔" "کیوں؟"

"کیونکہ اگر کھوٹی چونی کی بجائے کھوٹی اٹھنی چل جائے تو زیادہ فائدہ ہے۔"

"خوب خوب یہ دلیل واقعی مضبوط ہے۔ کھوٹی اٹھنی ہی لکھوں گا۔" ماسٹر رونق رام سے جان چھڑا کر آگے چلتا ہوں کہ ڈاکٹر بانکے بہاری راستہ گھیر لیتے ہیں "اخاہ پروفیسر صاحب، میں آپ کا ہی انتظار کر رہا تھا۔ مجھے معلوم ہے آپ اس وقت ضرور ادھر سے گذرتے ہیں۔ آیئے آپ کو تازہ افسانہ سناؤں۔ عنوان ہے۔ ہیضہ کا مریض۔" ڈاکٹر بانکے بہاری کو افسانے لکھنے کا شوق ہے۔ ویسے اگر آپ ان کے افسانے سنیں تو خدا کا شکر بجا لائیں کہ یہ ڈاکٹری کی جانب چلے گئے ورنہ افسانہ بیچارا کسی کو منھ نہ دکھا سکتا۔ اب ڈاکٹر صاحب نے اپنا طویل افسانہ پڑھنا شروع کر دیا یہ کوئی پچاس ساٹھ صفحوں پر پھیلا ہوا ہے وہ افسانہ پڑھ رہے ہیں اور میں یہ دیکھ رہا ہوں کہ ابھی کتنے صفحے اور باقی ہیں۔ جی کڑا کر کے کبھی کبھی داد بھی دیتا جاتا ہوں کہ ناراض نہ ہو جائیں۔ دس صفحے سننے کے بعد ہمت اور صبر جواب دے دیتے ہیں اس لئے جلدی سے ان سے معذرت کر کے ان کے کمرے سے بھاگتا ہوں۔

لیجئے ابھی چند قدم ہی چل سکا ہوں کہ شری شمبھو ناتھ نے اپنی مہین آواز میں پکارتے ہوئے کہا "میں نے کہا جی ذرا بات تو سنئے۔" شری شمبھو ناتھ ریٹائرڈ کلرک ہیں۔ ساٹھ پینسٹھ کے قریب عمر ہے ہمیشہ پانچ چھ امراض میں مبتلا رہتے ہیں۔ لیجئے انھوں نے مجھے دیکھتے ہی اپنی گردن کی پشت پر ہاتھ مارتے ہوئے کہا کل رات سے یہاں درد ہو رہا ہے اس کا کیا کروں؟ "کسی ڈاکٹر کو دکھائیے۔" "ڈاکٹر کو دکھایا ہے اس کی سمجھ میں کچھ نہیں آیا۔" "تو کسی حکیم یا وید سے مشورہ کیجئے۔" "وید سے بھی مشورہ کیا ہے۔" "تو پھر ٹھیک ہے۔" "نہیں ٹھیک ہے۔ درد بدستور ہے۔ آپ بتائیے کہ کیا جائے؟" "تیل کی مالش کیجئے۔" "وہ تو کی ہے۔" "سینک دیجئے۔" "وہ تو دیا ہے۔" "تو پھر اس پر برف کی تھیلی رکھئے۔"

"اجی پروفیسر صاحب۔ آپ تو مذاق کرتے ہیں۔ اچھا چھوڑیئے۔ چند دنوں سے بدہضمی کی شکایت ہے۔ رات کو نیند نہیں آتی۔ آنکھیں سوج رہی ہیں۔ پیٹ پھول رہا ہے۔ اس کا بتائیے کیا کیا جائے۔" اب آپ ہی کہیئے کہ شری شمبھو ناتھ کے لئے کونسا نسخہ تجویز کیا جائے۔ اور خاص کر جب معاملہ یہ ہو کہ خاکسار پروفیسر تو ضرور ہے لیکن ڈاکٹر بالکل نہیں۔ "لالہ جی تر پھلا پھانکا کیجئے۔" میں نے آہستہ سے کہا۔ اور ان سے اجازت لیتا ہوں۔ ہانپتے کانپتے ڈاک خانے پہنچتا ہوں۔ لیکن ڈاک کب کی جا چکی ہے۔ مایوس ہو کر گھر کی طرف لوٹتا ہوں اور سوچ رہا ہوں کہ اگر واپسی پر پھر شری شمبھو ناتھ ڈاکٹر بانکے بہاری، ماسٹر رنبھی رام یا صوبیدار صاحب سے تصادم ہو گیا تو آدھی رات سے پہلے گھر نہیں پہنچ سکتا۔

دانت نکلوانا

شیکسپیئر نے ایک جگہ لکھا ہے کہ شاکر سے شاکر انسان بھی دانت کا درد برداشت نہیں کر سکتا۔ اس فقرے کی صداقت کو صرف وہی لوگ محسوس کر سکتے ہیں جن کو شیکسپیئر یا میری طرح کبھی دانت کا درد ہوا ہو۔ ورنہ عام انسان تو اس فقرے کو پڑھ کر بے اختیار مسکرا دیتا ہے اور کہتا ہے۔ یہ شیکسپیئر بھی کتنا سادہ لوح آدمی تھا۔ اگر دانت کے درد کی بجائے تولنج کا درد۔ یا جگر کا درد لکھ دیتا تو شاید میں مان جاتا۔ مگر دانت کا درد!۔۔۔۔ حتےٰ کہ کسی دن اس کو اچانک رات کے گیارہ بجے دانت کا درد آ دباتا ہے۔ پہلے پہلے وہ شاکر بننے اور شیکسپیئر کو جھٹلانے کی ناکام کوشش کرتا ہے اور دل کو یوں تسلی دیتا ہے کہ آخر غالب مرحوم نے بھی تو فرمایا ہے کہ "درد کا حد سے گذرنا ہے دوا ہو جانا"۔ پھر خواہ مخواہ پریشان ہونے کی کیا ضرورت ہے۔ مگر جب دو دن کے بعد یہ درد اسے رات کو

مطلقاً سونے نہیں دیتا۔ اور اس کی وجہ سے وہ گھر میں کسی اور کو مطلقاً سونے نہیں دیتا۔ تو اسے شیکسپیئر کی بات کا کچھ کچھ یقین ہونے لگتا ہے۔ اور تیسرے دن علی الصبح وہ اپنے آپ کو کسی دندان ساز کے ویٹنگ روم میں بیٹھا ہوا پاتا ہے۔

بعینہ یہی حال پچھلے ہفتہ میرا ہوا۔ ویسے تو میں تقریباً ہر درد سے آشنا ہوں۔ مگر یہ معلوم نہ تھا کہ دانت کے درد میں وہ تڑپ پوشیدہ ہے کہ دردِ دل، دردِ گردہ، دردِ جگر تو اسکے مقابلے میں 'عین راحت' ہیں۔ چنانچہ جب متواتر تین رات کراہنے اور ہمسائے کے تجربے سے فائدہ اٹھانے کے بعد بھی درد میں کچھ افاقہ نہ ہوا تو میں نے ڈاکٹر اندر کمار کی دوکان کا رخ کیا۔ آپ دانتوں کی بیماریوں کے ماہر ہیں۔ اور دانت بجلی سے نکالتے ہیں۔ شاید موخرالذکر چیز نے مجھے ان کی جانب رجوع کرنے کو اکسایا۔ کیونکہ درد اس حد تک پہنچ چکا تھا کہ بجلی کے سوا شاید ہی کوئی دوسری چیز مجھے بچا سکتی۔ چنانچہ میں نے ان کی دوکان میں لپکتے ہوئے کہا۔ "میری بائیں داڑھ فوراً بجلی سے نکال دیجئے۔" ڈاکٹر صاحب نے حیرت سے میری طرف تکتے ہوئے کہا۔ "آپ کہاں سے تشریف لائے ہیں؟" میں نے کہا۔ "آپ مجھ سے راہ و رسم بعد میں بڑھا سکتے ہیں۔ پہلے میری بائیں داڑھ نکالئے۔" ڈاکٹر صاحب نے کہا۔ "تشریف رکھئے۔ گھبرانے کی ضرورت نہیں۔ ابھی نکالے دیتا ہوں۔" اس کے بعد آپ نے مجھ پر سوالات کی بھرمار ہی شروع کر دی۔ مثلاً "کب سے درد ہے؟ کیوں درد ہے؟ اوپر والی داڑھ میں ہے یا نیچے والی داڑھ میں؟ اس سے پہلے بھی کبھی دانت نکلوایا ہے؟ کیا صرف ایک ہی دانت نکلوانا چاہتے ہیں؟

اب میں تھا کہ درد سے بیتاب ہو رہا تھا اور ہر سوال کا جواب دینے کی مجھ میں ہمت نہ تھی۔ مگر ڈاکٹر صاحب تھے کہ برابر مسکرائے جا رہے تھے۔ اور جب میں درد سے کراہتا تو ان کی مسکراہٹ زیادہ دلآویز اور دلکش ہو جاتی۔ آخر جب انھوں نے دو تین دفعہ میرے منع کرنے کے باوجود اچھی طرح داڑھ کو ہلایا اور دیکھا کہ شدت درد سے مجھ پر بیہوشی طاری ہوا چاہتی ہے تو انھیں یقین ہو گیا کہ واقعی دانت کا درد ہے۔ اس کے بعد انھوں نے مجھے کرسی پر بیٹھنے کا اشارہ کیا۔ اور خود دو تین اوزار گرم پانی میں ابالنے لگے۔ میں نے کہا۔ "ذرا حضرت جلدی کیجئے۔ بجلی سے میری داڑھ نکالئے" کہنے لگے۔ "آج بجلی خراب ہو گئی ہے۔ اس لئے داڑھ ہاتھ سے ہی نکالنا پڑے گی۔

جتنا عرصہ اوزار گرم ہوتے رہے۔ وہ مجھے دانت کی خرابیوں سے پیدا ہونیوالی بیماریوں پر لیکچر دیتے رہے۔ ان کے خیال کے مطابق دنیا کی تمام بیماریاں دانتوں ہی کے خراب ہو جانے سے پیدا ہوتی ہیں۔ چنانچہ بدہضمی سے تپ دق تک جتنے امراض ہیں ان کا علاج داڑھ نکلوانا ہے۔ اس لیکچر میں آپ نے اس ملک کے لوگوں کی عادات پر بھی کچھ تبصرہ کیا۔ مثلاً یہاں کے لوگ بے حد بے پرواہ واقع ہوئے ہیں۔ امریکہ اور انگلینڈ میں ہر ایک آدمی سال میں چار دفعہ دانت صاف کرواتا ہے۔ مگر یہاں لوگ اس وقت تک دندان ساز کی دوکان کا رخ نہیں کرتے جب تک دانت کو کیڑا لگ کر سارا مسوڑہ تباہ نہ ہو جائے افسوس تو اس بات کا ہے کہ آپ جیسے پڑھے لکھے آدمی بھی دانتوں کی ذرا پرواہ نہیں کرتے۔ اگر لوگ ذرا احتیاط ہوں تو آج ان کی مشکلیں حل ہو جائیں۔

اس قسم کے متعدد جملے وہ ایک ہی سانس میں کہہ گئے۔ حتیٰ کہ مجھے محسوس ہونے لگا کہ ہمارے ملک کے سچے خیر خواہ صرف آپ ہیں۔ اور اگر آپ نہ ہوتے تو خدا جانے ہمارے ملک کی کیا حالت ہوتی۔

جب اورزار گرم ہو چکے تو ڈاکٹر صاحب نے فرمایا۔ اب انجکشن ہوگا۔ انجکشن کے نام سے مجھے روزِ اول ہی سے چڑ ہے۔ کیونکہ میرے خیال میں انجکشن مہذب طریقے سے ایذا پہنچانے کا دوسرا نام ہے۔ مگر ڈاکٹر صاحب نے یقین دلایا کہ انجکشن سے کسی قسم کا درد نہیں ہوگا۔ بعد میں مجھے معلوم ہوا کہ وہ کسی قدر مبالغہ آمیزی سے کام لے رہے تھے۔ کیونکہ انجکشن سے کافی درد ہوا۔ انجکشن کرنے کے دو تین منٹ بعد انھوں نے زنبور پکڑا۔ اور اب مجھے وہ انسان کی بجائے موت کا فرشتہ نظر آنے لگے۔ دل میں آیا کہ ہمت کر کے بھاگ نکلوں۔ میں اٹھا ہی چاہتا تھا کہ انھوں نے ذرا نرمی سے کہا "میں آپ کو بارھویں دفعہ پھر یقین دلاتا ہوں کہ آپ کو مطلقاً درد نہیں ہوگا۔" میں نے دبی زبان سے کہا "میں آپ کو بارھویں دفعہ یقین دلاتا ہوں کہ مجھے آپ کی بات کا یقین نہیں۔" مگر انھوں نے معاملے کو طول نہ دیتے ہوئے مجھے منہ کھولنے کو کہا۔ وہ داڑھ کو زنبور کی گرفت میں لائے اور مجھے محسوس ہوا کہ اب وصیت کرنے اور احباب اور اقربا کو آخری تلقین کرنے کا وقت آپہونچا۔ انھوں نے زنبور کو جھٹکا دیا اور درد حد سے گذر کر قضا معلوم ہونے لگا۔ انھوں نے دوسرا جھٹکا دیا اور میں سمجھا کہ اب انھوں نے مجھے ضرور جان سے مارنے کا فیصلہ کر لیا ہے۔ اس کے بعد دانت اور زنبور کی ایک باقاعدہ کشتی شروع ہوئی۔ داڑھ اپنی جگہ پر اس طرح قائم تھی جس طرح

قطب مینار ہزاروں زلزلوں کے باوجود اب تک اپنی جگہ پر جما ہوا ہے۔ مگر اس کھینچا تانی میں میں مفت میں ذبح ہو رہا تھا۔ یہ کشتی یا کش مکش کافی عرصہ تک جاری رہی اور آخر زنبور اور دانت میں یہ تصفیہ ہوا کہ آدھی داڑھ زنبور کے منہ میں اور آدھی میرے منہ میں رہے۔ ڈاکٹر صاحب اس وقت پسینہ پسینہ ہوئے تھے ان کی گھبراہٹ دیکھ کر قریب تھا کہ میں بھی ہوش وحواس کھو بیٹھوں کہ انھوں نے بناوٹی مسکراہٹ کے ساتھ فرمایا "تو یہ کتنی گہرائی میں ہے یہ داڑھ۔ بہت کوشش کی کہ نہ ٹوٹے۔ مگر ٹوٹ ہی گئی۔"

درد سے کراہتے ہوئے میں نے کہا۔ "اب کیا ہوگا؟"

"گھبرانے کی ضرورت نہیں۔"

اس کے بعد انھوں نے جس طرح میری باقی کی آدھی داڑھ نکالی۔ یہ صرف وہی لوگ جان سکتے ہیں جنھیں دانت ٹوٹنے کا سانحہ کبھی پیش آیا ہو۔ بس صرف یہ سمجھ لیجئے کہ میری وہی حالت تھی جو آپ کی ہو۔ اگر میں آپ کے بدن میں متعدد جگہوں سے لمبی لمبی سوئیاں چبھوتا جاؤں اور ساتھ ساتھ آپ کو تسلی دیتا رہوں کہ گھبرانے کی کوئی ضرورت نہیں۔ تقریباً آدھ گھنٹے کی پیہم کوشش کے بعد ڈاکٹر صاحب باقی ڈاڑھ نکالنے میں کامیاب ہو گئے۔

اس عرصے میں مجھے ایسا معلوم ہوا کہ کئی بار اگلے جہان پہنچا ہوں اور کئی بار وہاں سے لوٹا ہوں۔ اور پھر آخر کار میں نے اپنے آپ کو نیم بسمل کی سی حالت میں ڈاکٹر صاحب کی کرسی میں بیٹھا ہوا پایا۔ جب کچھ ہوش سنبھالا۔ تو ایسا معلوم ہوا کہ منہ سے بے تحاشا خون بہہ رہا ہے اور ڈاکٹر صاحب ایک

گلاس لیکر جس میں خون سے ملتی جلتی رنگت والی کوئی دوا گھلی ہوئی ہے۔ کرسی کے نزدیک کھڑے ہیں۔ اس کے بعد چند لمحے نہایت عذاب کی حالت میں گذرے ڈاکٹر صاحب غرارے کرنے کو کہہ رہے تھے اور میں انھیں ایمبولنس کار کے لئے فون کرنے کو عرض کر رہا تھا اور ساتھ ہی سوچ رہا تھا کہ اسی حالت میں اٹھ کر نزدیک کے پولیس اسٹیشن میں جاکر اس سانحہ کی ۔ رپورٹ درج کراؤں تو شاید ضرورت کے وقت کام آئے۔ بارے کہیں پندرہ منٹ کے بعد خون بہنا بند ہوا ۔ کچھ ڈھارس بندھی ۔ مگر اب سخت درد ہونا شروع ہوا اور میں نے بہتری اسی میں سمجھی کہ ڈاکٹر صاحب کی دکان میں بے گور و کفن مرنے کی نسبت گھر لوٹ چلوں تانگہ میں بیٹھ کر بڑی مشکل سے گھر پہنچا اور ایک گھنٹہ تک اوندھے منہ بستر میں لیٹا کراہتا رہا۔ اس کے بعد جوں جوں درد کم ہوتا گیا ۔ گال سوجتا گیا ۔ حتیٰ کہ دو تین گھنٹے کے بعد مجھے ایسا معلوم ہونے لگا ۔ گویا میرے جسم پر کسی اور شخص کا چہرہ لگا ہوا ہے۔ اس وقت میں سمجھا کہ کیوں میرے ہموطن دندان ساز کی دکان کا آسانی سے رخ نہیں کرتے ۔

مجھے میرے بزرگوں سے بچاؤ!

میں ایک چھوٹا سا لڑکا ہوں۔ ایک بہت بڑے گھر میں رہتا ہوں۔ دراصل رہتا کہاں ہوں۔ زندگی کے دن کاٹتا ہوں۔ چونکہ سب سے چھوٹا ہوں اس لئے گھر میں سب میرے بزرگ کہلاتے ہیں۔ یہ سب مجھ سے بے انتہا محبت کرتے ہیں۔ انھیں چاہے اپنی صحت کا خیال رہے نہ رہے میری صحت کا خیال ضرور ستاتا رہتا ہے۔ داداجی کو ہی لیجئے۔ یہ مجھے گھر سے باہر نکلنے نہیں دیتے کیونکہ باہر گرمی یا برف پڑ رہی ہے۔ بارش ہو رہی ہے یا درختوں کے پتے جھڑ رہے ہیں کیا معلوم کوئی پتہ میرے سر پر تڑاخ سے لگے اور میری کھوپڑی پھوٹ جائے۔ ان کے خیال میں گھر اچھا خاصا قید خانہ ہونا چاہیئے۔ ان کا بس چلے تو ہر ایک گھر کو جس میں بچے رہتے ہیں سینٹرل جیل میں تبدیل کر کے رکھدیں۔ وہ فرماتے ہیں کہ بچوں کو بزرگوں کی خدمت کرنا چاہیئے۔ یہی وجہ ہے کہ ہر وقت مجھ سے

چلم بھرواتے یا پاؤں دبواتے رہتے ہیں۔

دادی جی بہت اچھی ہیں۔ پوپلا منھ۔ چہرے پر بیشمار جھریاں، اور خیالات بے حد پرانے۔ یہ ہر وقت مجھے بھوتوں، جنوں اور چڑیلوں کی باتیں سنا سنا کر ڈراتی رہتی ہیں "دیکھو بیٹا۔ مندر کے پاس جو پیپل ہے، اس کے نیچے مت کھیلنا۔ اس کے اوپر ایک بھوت رہتا ہے۔ آج سے پچاس برس پہلے جب ابھی میری شادی نہیں ہوئی تھی۔ میں اپنی سہیلی کے ساتھ اس پیپل کی چھاؤں میں کھیل رہی تھی کہ یک لخت میری سہیلی بے ہوش ہوگئی۔ جب اسے ہوش آیا تو اس نے چیخ کر کہا۔ "بھوت" اور وہ پھر بے ہوش ہوگئی۔ اس طرح وہ سات دفعہ ہوش میں آئی اور سات دفعہ بیہوش ہوئی۔ اسے گھر پہنچایا گیا جہاں وہ سات دن کے بعد مر گئی۔" "اور ہاں پرانی سرائے میں جو کنواں ہے اس کے نزدیک مت پھٹکنا۔ اس میں ایک چڑیل رہتی ہے۔ وہ بچوں کا کلیجہ نکال کر کھا جاتی ہے۔ اس چڑیل کی یہی خوراک ہے۔"

پتا جی کا تکیہ کلام ہے: "نالائق" ایک اور تکیہ کلام ہے: "جب میں طالب علم تھا" وہ جب بھی مجھ سے گفتگو کرتے ہیں۔ ان دونوں میں سے ایک تکیہ کلام کا ضرور استعمال کرتے ہیں۔

"آج کتنے سوال نکالے؟"

"جی دس۔"

"صرف دس۔ نالائق۔"

"آج تاریخ کے کتنے صفحے پڑھے؟"

"جی ہیں"

"نالائق۔ جب میں طالب علم تھا۔ پچاس صفحے پڑھا کرتا تھا"

"اکبر کون تھا"

"جی ایک بادشاہ تھا"

"نالائق۔ کہو ایک بہت اچھا بادشاہ تھا"

"امتحان میں کیسے رہے"

"جی جماعت میں تیسرا رہا ہوں"

"نالائق۔ جب میں طالب علم تھا۔ ہمیشہ اوّل آیا کرتا تھا"

"آج کتنی روٹیاں کھائیں"

"جی تین"

"نالائق۔ جب میں طالب علم تھا۔ دس روٹیاں کھایا کرتا تھا"

ماتاجی کو ہر وقت یہ خدشہ لگا رہتا ہے کہ پرماتما نہ کرے اگر مجھے کچھ ہو گیا تو پھر کیا ہوگا۔ وہ مجھے تالاب میں تیرنے کے لئے اس لئے نہیں جانے دیتیں کہ اگر میں ڈوب گیا تو؟ آتشبازی کے انار وں۔ پٹاخوں اور پھلجھڑیوں سے اس لئے کھیلنے نہیں دیتیں کہ اگر میرے کپڑوں میں آگ لگ گئی تو! خالی پستول کو ہاتھ میں لینے کی اجازت نہیں دیتیں کہ اگر یہ چل گیا تو؟ پچھلے دنوں میں کرکٹ کھیلنا چاہتا تھا۔ ماتاجی کو پتہ لگ گیا۔ کہنے لگیں۔ "کرکٹ مت کھیلنا۔ بڑا خطرناک کھیل ہے۔ پرماتما نہ کرے اگر گیند آنکھ پر لگ گئی تو؟"

بڑے بھائی صاحب کا خیال ہے کہ جو چیز بڑوں کے لئے بے ضرر ہے

چھوٹوں کے لئے سخت مضر ہے۔ خود چوبیس گھنٹے پان کھاتے ہیں۔ لیکن اگر مجھے کبھی پان کھاتے ہوئے دیکھ لیں تو فوراً ناک بھوں چڑھا کر کہیں گے "پان نہیں کھانا چاہیئے۔ بہت گندی عادت ہے" سینما دیکھنے کے بہت شوقین ہیں۔ لیکن میں اگر ساتھ جانے پر اصرار کروں تو کہیں گے "چھوٹوں کو فلمیں نہیں دیکھنا چاہیئں اخلاق پر بہت برا اثر پڑتا ہے"۔

اسی طرح چھوٹوں کو عطر نہیں لگانا چاہیئے تاکہ ان کے کپڑوں سے خوشبو نہ آئے۔ نظمیں (نہیں) لکھنا چاہیئے تاکہ وہ بڑے ہوکر شاعر نہ بن جائیں۔ ہنسنا نہیں چاہیئے۔ تاکہ وہ ہمیشہ اداس رہیں۔

اب رہیں ہماری بھابی۔ انھیں افسانے لکھنے اور جاسوسی ناول پڑھنے کا شوق ہے۔ ان کا تکیہ کلام ہے "لپک کے جائیو" جب بھی میں کمر سیدھی کرنے کے لئے لیٹتا ہوں وہ کہتی ہیں۔ "لپک کے جائیو اور رول اینڈ بک شاپ سے رسالہ "سورج مکھی" کا تازہ نمبر لے آئیو۔ اگر "سورج مکھی" نہ ملے تو "چندر مکھی" لے آنا۔ اگر وہ بھی نہ آیا ہو تو "تارا مکھی"۔ اور ہاں پوچھتے آنا کہ نیلا لاک چین کا دوسرا حصہ چھپ کر آگیا یا نہیں۔ اور پھر "نیلا ڈاکو" کب تک چھپ رہا ہے"۔ سارا دن ایک بک شاپ سے دوسرے بک اسٹال تک مارا مارا پھرتا ہوں۔ کبھی "نقاب پوش" حصہ اول کی تلاش میں، کبھی "پراسرار قلعہ حصہ دوم" کی کھوج میں۔

بڑی بہن کو گانے بجانے کا شوق ہے۔ ان کی فرمائشیں اس قسم کی ہوتی ہیں۔ "ہارمونیم پھر خراب ہوگیا ہے اسے ٹھیک کرالاؤ۔ ستار کے دو تار ٹوٹ گئے ہیں اسے میوزیکل ہاؤس لے جاؤ۔ طبلہ بڑی خوفناک آوازیں نکالنے

لگتا ہے اسے فلاں دوکان پر چھوڑ آؤں۔" جب انہیں کوئی کام لینا ہو تو بڑی میٹھی بن جاتی ہیں۔ کام نہ ہو تو کاٹنے کو دوڑتی ہیں۔ خاص کر جب ان کی سہیلیاں آتی ہیں اور وہ طرح طرح کی فضول باتیں بناتی ہیں اس وقت میں انہیں زہر لگنے لگتا ہوں۔

لے دے کے سارے گھر میں ایک غم گسار ہے اور وہ ہے میرا کتا "موتی" بڑا شریف جانور ہے۔ وہ نہ تو بھوتوں اور چڑیلوں کے قصے سنا کر مجھے خوفزدہ کرنے کی کوشش کرتا ہے نہ مجھے نالائق کہہ کر میری حوصلہ شکنی کرتا ہے اور نہ اسے جاسوسی ناول پڑھنے کا شوق ہے نہ ستار بجانے کا۔ بس ذرا موج میں آئے تو تھوڑا سا بھونک لیتا ہے۔ جب اپنے بزرگوں سے تنگ آجاتا ہوں تو اسے ساتھ لے کر جنگل میں نکل جاتا ہوں۔ وہاں ہم دونوں تیتریوں کے پیچھے بھاگتے ہیں۔ گلہریوں کا تعاقب کرتے ہیں۔ چشمے میں ناچتی ہوئی مچھلیوں کو دیکھتے ہیں۔ دادا جی اور دادی جی سے دور۔ پتا جی اور ماتا جی سے دور۔ بھابی اور بہن کی دسترس سے دور۔ اور کبھی کبھی کسی درخت کی گھنی چھاؤں میں موتی کے ساتھ ستاتے ہوئے میں سوچنے لگتا ہوں۔" کاش! میرے بزرگ سمجھ سکتے کہ میں بھی انسان ہوں۔ یا کاش وہ اتنی جلدی بھول نہ جاتے کہ وہ کبھی میری طرح ایک چھوٹا سا لڑکا ہوا کرتے تھے؟

"چندا رے!"

کردار:۔

پروفیسر راکیش

بھولا: پروفیسر راکیش کا نوکر

چندا: خاتون فاتون فائن آرٹس سوسائٹی کی سیکریٹری

نیلا امبر اور رشی: پروفیسر راکیش کے دو بے تکلف دوست

مقام:۔

پروفیسر راکیش کا ڈرائنگ روم

پروفیسر راکیش: (ایک کتاب کا مطالعہ کرتے ہوئے) آہا ہا! کتنا دلچسپ مجموعہ ہے! اور پھر نام کتنا پیارا ہے: چندا رے! لطف یہ

کہ یہ سب گیت چندا پر لکھے گئے ہیں۔ چندا رے تو روتا کیوں ہے۔
چندا رے تو کیوں مسکائے ؟ چندا رے کیا صبح نہ ہوگی
چندا رے تو کیوں شرمائے ؟ چندا رے تو کیوں چندا ہے ؟
یہ فلمی شاعر بھی کمال کرتے ہیں۔ چندا کیا سوال کیا ہے۔ کہ چندا رے
تو کیوں چندا ہے ؟ اب بھلا بے چارا چندا اس سوال کا کیا جواب
دے گا۔ اور پھر یہ گیت کہ چندا رے او ظالم چندا۔ (نوکر کو آواز
دیتے ہوئے) بھولا۔ ارے بھولا۔

بھولا : جی سرکار۔
راکیش: ذرا ادھر آؤ۔
بھولا : (قریب آتے ہوئے) جی سرکار
راکیش: بھولا۔ کیا تم جانتے ہو کہ چندا کیوں ظالم چندا ہے۔
بھولا : سرکار اپنے دھندے سے فرصت ہی کتنی ملتی ہے کہ بندہ یہ سوچے
کہ چندا کیوں ظالم چندا ہے۔
راکیش: تم ایک دم ڈل (Dull) ہو بھولا۔ ایک دم ڈل۔ فلمی گیت سمجھنا
تمہارے بس کا روگ نہیں۔ اچھا تم جاؤ۔ ہم سوچتے ہیں آج کالج
سے چھٹی ہے ۔ ۔ ۔ ۔ ہاں بازار سے دو درجن سگرٹ لے آؤ۔
بھولا : بہت اچھا سرکار۔ (جاتا ہے)
راکیش: ہم۔ چندا رے او ظالم چندا۔ شاید چندا اس لئے ظالم ہے کہ وہ
سوسج نہیں ہے یا شاید اس لئے کہ وہ شاعر کو ظالم نظر آتا ہے۔

یہ بھی ہو سکتا ہے کہ چندا اس لئے ظالم ہے کہ شاعر کا محبوب اس سے روٹھ گیا ہے اور اسے اس کی یاد ستا رہی ہے۔ ہُم۔ لیکن یہ بات کیا بنی۔ **او چندا ئے او ظالم چندا۔**

(کوئی دروازہ کھٹ کھٹاتا ہے)

راکیش: کون؟

آواز: جی میں ہوں چندا۔

راکیش: (حیرانی سے) چندا! لیکن تم آسمان سے زمین پر کیسے آ گئے؟ خیر دروازہ کھلا ہے۔ تشریف لے آئیے۔

چندا: (کمرے میں داخل ہوتے ہوئے) نمستے۔

راکیش: نمستے۔

چندا: میں فائن فائن فائن آرٹس سوسائٹی کی سکریٹری ہوں۔

راکیش: یہ فائن فائن فائن آرٹس کیا بلا ہے؟

چندا: یہ ایک نئی سوسائٹی ہے۔ اس کا مقصد فائن آرٹس بالخصوص پینٹنگ کو فروغ دینا ہے۔ اس سوسائٹی کے جتنے ممبر ہیں وہ پینٹنگ میں عجیب غریب تجربے کر رہے ہیں۔ وہ چاہتے ہیں کہ ایسی تصویریں بنائی جائیں جن کو دیکھ کر بدن کے رونگٹے کھڑے ہو جائیں۔

راکیش: خوب۔ بہت خوب! اچھا تو آپ کے پاس ایسی تصاویر ہیں جنھیں دیکھ کر۔۔۔۔۔؟

چندا: "جی ہاں! یہ دیکھئے میرا البم! اس میں میری تازہ ترین تصاویر ہیں۔"
راکیش: دکھائیے ذرا۔
چندا: (البم کھول کر ایک تصویر دکھاتے ہوئے) یہ پہلی تصویر ملاحظہ فرمائیے
اس کا نام ہے: "بندرابن کی گوپی"
راکیش: (تصویر کو غور سے دیکھتے ہوئے) بندرابن کی گوپی؟ مجھے تو گوپی وپی کہیں نظر نہیں آتی۔ یہ تو ایسا لگتا ہے کہ آپ نے ایک بڑے کاشی پھل کے اوپر ایک چھوٹا کاشی پھل رکھ کر اس کے اوپر کوئلے کے دو ٹکڑے رکھ دئے ہیں۔
چندا: (ہنستے ہوئے) ہاہاہا۔ واہ پروفیسر صاحب۔ آپ جیسا سمجھدار آدمی بھی دھوکا کھا گیا۔ اجی جسے آپ بڑا کاشی پھل سمجھ رہے ہیں وہ گوپی کا پیٹ ہے۔ اور وہ جو چھوٹا کاشی پھل ہے وہ اس کا سر ہے اور یہ کوئلے کے دو ٹکڑے نہیں۔ گوپی کی چمکتی ہوئی آنکھیں ہیں۔
راکیش: ہُم۔ یہ بات ہے۔ اچھا ذرا دوسری تصویر دکھیں۔
چندا: ہاں یہ دوسری تصویر ہے۔ بھلا بتائیے یہ کیا ہے۔
راکیش: کچھ کہہ نہیں سکتا کہ یہ کیا ہے۔ معلوم تو یہی ہوتا ہے کہ یہ ایک بندر ہاتھ میں خربوزہ پکڑ کر کوئیں میں اترنے کی کوشش کر رہا ہے۔
چندا: واہ پروفیسر صاحب خوب سمجھے، اجی یہ بندر نہیں مستقبل کا انسان ہے اس کے ہاتھ میں خربوزہ نہیں، ایٹم بم ہے اور وہ جو کنواں ہے کنواں نہیں تباہی کا غار ہے، سمجھے آپ؟

راکیش: سمجھا تو نہیں لیکن چونکہ آپ ایسا کہتی ہیں اس لئے مان لیتا ہوں۔

چندا: دراصل یہ آپ کا قصور نہیں۔ یہ ہم آرٹسٹوں کا قصور ہے، ہم آپ کو ایسی تصاویر بہت کم تعداد میں دے رہے ہیں اس لئے آپ انھیں سمجھنے سے قاصر ہیں۔ آپ بھی بہت سے اور لوگوں کی طرح وہی تصاویر پسند کرتے ہیں جنھیں دیکھ کر کچھ سوچنا نہ پڑے۔

راکیش: یہ تو آپ بجا فرماتی ہیں۔ اچھا یہ بتائیے کہ آپ یہاں تشریف کیسے لائیں۔ اگر آپ چاہتی ہیں کہ میں ان تصاویر پر ایک آدھ مضمون لکھوں تو یہ مجھ سے نہ ہوگا۔ کیونکہ جس چیز کو میں سمجھ نہیں سکتا اس کے متعلق کبھی نہیں لکھتا۔

چندا: جی نہیں، یہ بات نہیں۔ میں آپ سے اپنی سوسائٹی کے لئے چندہ لینے آئی ہوں۔

راکیش: چندہ؟

چندا: جی ہاں چندہ۔ دیکھئے ہمارے بہت سے آرٹسٹ بھوکوں مر رہے ہیں۔ ایک کو پچھلے چھ ماہ سے کالی کھانسی کی شکایت ہے۔ ڈاکٹر کا خیال ہے کہ اسے بہت جلد دق ہو جائے گی۔ دوسرے کا دماغ چل گیا ہے اسے پاگل خانے بھجوانا پڑے گا۔ تیسرے کی آنکھوں میں موتیا بند اتر آیا ہے، اس کا آپریشن ہوگا۔ کہنے کا مطلب یہ ہے کہ روپے کی اشد ضرورت ہے۔

راکیش: اگر روپے کی ضرورت ہے تو آپ ان آرٹسٹوں کی تصاویر فروخت

کر کے روپیہ حاصل کر سکتی ہیں۔

چندا : وہ تو ٹھیک ہے۔ لیکن مصیبت یہ ہے کہ کوئی شخص ان کی تصاویر خریدنا نہیں چاہتا۔

راکیش : اور خریدے بھی کیوں۔ جبکہ ان تصاویر کا سر ہے نہ پیر۔

چندا : یہ بات نہیں پروفیسر صاحب۔ دراصل لوگوں کا مذاق اتنا بگڑ چکا ہے کہ وہ ان تصاویر کی قدر نہیں کر سکتے۔ خیر یہ سب ٹھیک ہو جائے گا ہم کوشش کر رہے ہیں۔ ۔ ۔ ۔ اچھا تو کہئے کتنے روپے دے رہے ہیں آپ؟

راکیش : آج مہینے کی ۲۰ تاریخ ہے۔ اور میرے بٹوے میں صرف بیس روپے ہیں۔

چندا : (مایوسی سے) یہ تو بہت تھوڑے ہیں۔ میرا خیال تھا کہ آپ جیسا آرٹ کو سمجھنے والا کم از کم چالیس روپے تو دے گا۔

راکیش : معاف کیجئے۔ نہ تو میں اس قسم کے آرٹ کو سمجھتا ہوں اور نہ ہی چالیس روپے دے سکتا ہوں۔

چندا : اچھا تو بیس ہی لائیے۔

راکیش : میں آپ کو دے دوں، اور میں خود ۔ ۔ ۔ ۔ ؟

چندا : اچھا، پانچ رکھ لیجئے۔ میرا مطلب ہے۔ سگرٹ پان وغیرہ کے لئے اور پندرہ دے دیجئے۔

راکیش : نہیں۔ پندرہ زیادہ ہیں۔

چندا : اچھا تو چودہ دے دیجئے۔ دیکھئے چودہ سے ایک کم نہ لوں گی۔ نکالئے
نکالئے، میں پرچی کاٹتی ہوں۔
راکیش: (بیدلی سے) ہیں تو یہ بھی زیادہ۔ لیکن خیر۔ لیجئے۔
(روپے دیتا ہے)
چندا : شکریہ۔ بہت بہت شکریہ۔ فائن۔ فائن۔ فائن آرٹس سوسائٹی آپ کا
یہ احسان کبھی نہیں بھولے گی۔ اچھا نمستے۔
راکیش: نمستے۔
(چندا جاتی ہے)
راکیش: عجیب لڑکی معلوم ہوتی ہے یہ چندا بھی۔ اب کچھ کچھ سمجھ میں آ رہا ہے کہ
شاعر نے یہ کیوں کہا۔ ع۔ چندا رے اوظالم چندا۔ اونہہ۔ فائن فائن
فائن آرٹس سوسائٹی کتنا فضول نام رکھا ہے۔

(کوئی پھر دروازہ کھٹ کھٹاتا ہے)
آواز : پروفیسر راکیش گھر پر ہیں۔
راکیش: (آواز پہچانتے ہوئے) کون نیلامبر، آؤ بھئی آؤ۔ دروازہ کھلا ہے۔
(نیلامبر اور ششی اندر آتے ہیں)
نیلامبر: ہیلو راکیش۔
ششی: ہیلو پروفیسر
راکیش: آؤ بھئی بیٹھو۔

نیلامبر: نہیں ہم بیٹھیں گے نہیں۔ بس کھڑے کھڑے بات کریں گے۔

راکیش: کیوں خیر تو ہے۔

نیلامبر: ہاں خیر ہی ہے ششی اور ہم نے ایک نئی مہم شروع کی ہے اس کا نام ہے۔ "ایٹ مور وٹامن پلیز"

"EAT MORE VITAMIN PLEASE"

"مہربانی کرکے اور وٹامن کھائیے"۔ تم جانتے ہو کہ آج کل مہموں کا زمانہ ہے۔ ہم نے سوچا ہے کہ ہم بھی کیوں نہ ایک مہم شروع کردیں۔

راکیش: لیکن اس کی کیا ضرورت تھی۔ میرا تو خیال ہے لوگ پہلے ہی کافی وٹامن کھاتے ہیں۔ میرا مطلب ہے امیر لوگ۔

ششی: بالکل غلط۔ دیکھئے اگر آپ وٹامن "اے" کھاتے، تو آپ کے چہرے کا رنگ ہلدی کی طرح پیلا نہ ہوتا۔

نیلامبر: اور اگر آپ وٹامن "سی" کھاتے تو آپ کے دانت اتنے کمزور نہ ہوتے۔

ششی: اور اگر آپ وٹامن "اے، بی، سی" کھاتے۔ تو آپ کا جسم اکہرا نہ ہوتا۔

راکیش: بھئی میرا جسم، میرا چہرہ، میرے دانت اچھے خاصے ہیں اور میرا خیال ہے کہ میں کافی وٹامن کھاتا ہوں۔

نیلامبر: نہیں نہیں بالکل نہیں۔ یہی تو آپ کی غلطی ہے، آپ بھی ہزاروں لوگوں کی طرح سمجھتے ہیں کہ آپ کافی وٹامن کھاتے ہیں۔ حالانکہ آپ

بہت کم وٹامن کھاتے ہیں۔ اچھا بھلا آپ نے کبھی کیلے کے چھلکے کھائے ہیں؟

راکیش: کیلے کے چھلکے؟ کیلے کے چھلکے کون کھا سکتا ہے۔

ششی: اجی پروفیسر صاحب، کھانے والے سب کھاتے ہیں۔ اچھا آپ نے کبھی شیشم کے پتے کھائے ہیں۔

راکیش: شیشم کے پتے؟ یہ تو کبھی نہیں کھائے۔ خدا وہ وقت نہ لائے کہ یہ کھانا پڑیں۔

ششی: اجی دعا کیجئے کہ خدا آپ کو عقل دے۔ اور آپ بہت جلد شیشم کے پتے کھانا شروع کر دیں۔ معلوم ہے، شیشم کے پتوں میں کتنے وٹامن ہوتے ہیں۔

راکیش: ہوتے ہوں گے۔ لیکن میں شیشم کے پتے.....

نیلامبر: اچھا چھوڑیئے۔ آپ نے کبھی سبز گھاس کھائی؟

راکیش: گھاس؟ کیا تم مجھے جانور سمجھتے ہو؟

نیلامبر: اجی نہیں۔ سبز گھاس وٹامن "اے" اور "بی" کا سب سے بڑا مخزن ہے۔ دیکھئے گھوڑے، ہرن، بیل سب گھاس کھاتے ہیں اور کتنے طاقتور ہوتے ہیں۔

راکیش: گستاخی معاف۔ میں گھاس نہیں کھا سکتا۔

ششی: اوہ پروفیسر۔ یو ڈونٹ نو وہاٹ یو آر مسنگ؟

"You dont know what you are Missing"

نیلامبر: آپ کو کم از کم دو سیر گھاس ضرور رکھانا چاہیئے۔

راکیش: یہ تو معاف ہی رکھیئے۔ اچھا یہ بتلائیے کہ آپ کی کیا خدمت کی جائے۔ سگرٹ، پیپن.... چائے!

ششی: یہ تکلفات رہنے دیجئے۔ دیکھئے اس مہم کو ہر دلعزیز بنانے کے لئے ہمیں روپے کی ضرورت ہے۔ آپ کھلے دل سے چندہ دیکر ہماری مدد کیجئے۔

راکیش: چندہ! لیکن آج تو مہینے کی ۲۰ تاریخ ہے، اور میرے بٹوے میں صرف چھ روپے رہ گئے ہیں۔

ششی: کوئی بات نہیں، کوئی بات نہیں۔ ہمیں چھ روپے ہی دے دیجئے۔

راکیش: چھ روپے تمھیں دے دوں اور میں کیا کروں۔

نیلامبر: آپ وٹامن کھائیے۔!!! سمجھے آپ

راکیش: اچھا تین روپے لے لیجئے۔

نیلامبر: تین روپے۔ اتنے بڑے پروفیسر سے صرف تین روپے، اتنی ضروری مہم کے لئے تین روپے۔ دیکھئے چھ سے ایک کم نہ ہوگا۔

راکیش: اچھا بھئی ضد نہ کرو۔ پانچ لے لو۔

نیلامبر: اچھا لائو۔ ایک روپے کا ادھار رہا۔

راکیش: (پانچ روپے کا نوٹ دیتے ہوئے) لیجئے۔

نیلامبر: شکریہ..... اچھا نمستے۔

ششی: نمستے۔

(نیلا مبرا در ششی جاتے ہیں)

راکیش: مہینے کی ۲۰ تاریخ اور جیب میں صرف ایک روپیہ۔

(دروازہ کھٹ کھٹایا جاتا ہے)

راکیش: (اونچی آواز سے) اگر آپ بھی چندہ لینے آئے ہیں تو سمجھ لیجیے کہ میں گھر پر نہیں ہوں۔

(کھٹ۔ کھٹ کھٹ کی آواز)

راکیش: کون ہے بھئی۔

بھولا: جی میں ہوں بھولا۔ سگرٹ لایا ہوں۔

راکیش: اوہ بھولا ــــ میں تو ڈر ہی گیا تھا۔ (بھولا سے) میں سمجھا کہ تم بھی چندہ ہو!

بھولا: چندا؟ کون چندا؟ کہیں وہی تو نہیں جس کے متعلق آپ مجھ سے پوچھ رہے تھے۔

راکیش: نہیں نہیں۔ یہ دوسرا چندہ ہے۔ اس چندہ نے تو آج کمر ہی توڑ کر رکھ دی ہے۔

بھولا: کیا مطلب سرکار؟

راکیش: کچھ نہیں۔ کچھ نہیں۔ اچھا کوئی مجھ سے ملنے آئے تو اسے اندر مت آنے دینا۔

بھولا: اسے کیا کہوں سرکار؟

راکیش: اسے کہو کہ جب سے چندا آسمان سے اڑ کر زمین پر آ گیا ہے، صاحب چندہ سے گھبرا کر پاتال میں چلے گئے ہیں۔

بھولا: یہ آپ کیا کہہ رہے ہیں سرکار!

راکیش: بھولا۔ تم نہیں جانتے۔ چندہ کتنا ظالم ہوتا ہے۔

بھولا: صاحب۔ میں ایک دم ڈل ہوں۔ چندا کو سمجھنا میرے بس کا روگ نہیں۔ اچھا تو ملاقاتیوں سے کیا کہہ دوں!

راکیش: وہی جو میں نے کہا ہے۔

بھولا: بہت اچھا سرکار، بہت اچھا۔

کلاوناش عرف ستیاناس

کردار :- سیٹھ دمڑی پرشاد ...... پروڈیوسر

دھوم کیتو ...... ڈائرکٹر

گھسیٹا رام ...... ہیرو

شنگار بیگم ...... ہیروئن

مرزا ابوڑم بیگ ...... افسانہ نویس

سرگم شکارپوری ...... شاعر

پہلا منظر

سیٹھ دمڑی پرشاد کا کمرہ

(سیٹھ دمڑی پرشاد اخبار پڑھ رہے ہیں۔ دھوم کیتو داخل ہوتا ہے)

دھوم کیتو: نمستے۔ سیٹھ صاحب!

دمڑی پرشاد: اخبار سے نظریں اٹھا کر بڑی بے رخی سے) نمستے

دھوم کیتو: مجھے پہچانا۔ سیٹھ دمڑی پرشاد جی؟

دمڑی پرشاد: (سر کو کھجلاتے ہوئے) ایسا معلوم ہوتا ہے کہ آپ کو کہیں دیکھا ہے۔

دھوم کیتو: (ہنس کر) واہ سیٹھ صاحب۔ اتنی جلدی بھول گئے! اجی میں وہی دھوم کیتو ہوں دھوم کیتو۔ میں آپ کے محلے میں چنا زور گرم بیچا کرتا تھا۔ یاد ہے۔

چنا چُر مر چُر مر بولے   بابو کھانے کو منہ کھولے
چنا کھاتے سب بنگالی   جن کی دھوتی ڈھیلی ڈھالی
چنا زور گرم بابو۔ میں لایا مزیدار۔ چنا زور گرم

دمڑی پرشاد: (پہچانتے ہوئے) اوہ! دھوم کیتو! بھئی خوب ملے۔ کہو چنا زور گرم کا کیا حال ہے۔

دھوم کیتو: اجی چنا زور گرم کو گولی ماریئے۔ اب تو آپ کی دعا سے بندہ فلم لائن میں ہے۔

دمڑی پرشاد: فلم لائن میں چنا زور گرم بیچتے ہو کیا۔

دھوم کیتو: جی نہیں۔ بندہ فلمیں ڈائرکٹ کرتا ہے۔ یعنی بندہ فلم ڈائرکٹر۔۔۔

دمڑی پرشاد: (حیرانی سے) فلم ڈائرکٹر! لیکن تم فلم ڈائرکٹر کیسے بن گئے؟

دھوم کیتو: دیکھئے چنا زور گرم بیچ بیچ کر جب تنگ آگیا تو میں ایک تھیٹر میں

گھنٹی بجانے پر ملازم ہو گیا۔ اس کے بعد رفتہ رفتہ اسی تھیٹر میں پردے کھینچنے لگا۔ وہاں سے جو ترقی کی تو دیواروں پر فلموں کے اشتہار لگانے لگا۔ پھر ایک فلم سٹوڈیو کا دربان بن گیا۔ اب کی بار جو چھلانگ لگائی تو اپنے کو اچھا خاصا ڈائرکٹر پایا۔

دمڑی پرشاد: خوب خوب۔ بہت خوب۔ تم نے تو واقعی کمال کر دیا۔ اچھا یہ کہو کہ تم نے کوئی فلم بھی ڈائرکٹ کی یا نہیں۔

دھوم کیتو: فلموں کی کچھ نہ پوچھئے۔ بس یہ سمجھ لیجئے کہ کوئی ہی کام کی فلم ہو گی جو میں نے ڈائرکٹ نہیں کی۔ "پان کا یکہ" میں نے ڈائرکٹ کی۔ "عکم کی بیگم" کا میں خالق ہوں۔ "اینٹ کا بادشاہ" بھی خاکسار نے بنایا اور ان دنوں "چڑیا کا غلام" فلمانے کی فکر میں ہوں۔

دمڑی پرشاد: خوب۔ خوب۔ تو یوں کہیئے کہ آپ نے قریب قریب ساری کی ساری تاش ہی فلما دی۔ معلوم ہوتا ہے کہ آپ کافی پتے باز ہیں۔

دھوم کیتو: آپ کی نوازش ہے۔ ورنہ بندہ کس قابل ہے۔

دمڑی پرشاد: اچھا۔ یہ کہیئے کہ فلم انڈسٹری میں منافع کی کیا گنجائش ہے۔

دھوم کیتو: گنجائش سی گنجائش! سیٹھ صاحب۔ فلم انڈسٹری تو سونے کی کان ہے۔ پانچ لاکھ لگاؤ، دس لاکھ کماؤ۔ دس لاکھ لگاؤ، بیس لاکھ کماؤ۔ چالیس لاکھ کماؤ۔ بس منٹوں میں ہی وارے نیارے ہو جاتے ہیں۔

دمڑی پرشاد : ہوں ! یہ بات ہے۔
دھوم کیتو : جی ہاں۔ بالکل ٹھیک عرض کر رہا ہوں۔
دمڑی پرشاد : اچھا سنو۔ پچھلے دنوں ہم نے مونگ پھلی کے بیوپار میں کافی روپیہ کمایا ہے۔ اگر ہم ایک فلم بنائیں تو کیسی رہے۔
دھوم کیتو : بس یہ سمجھ لیجئے کہ چھ مہینے کے اندر اندر آپ دمڑی پرشاد سے کروڑی پرشاد بن جائیں گے۔
دمڑی پرشاد : واقعی !
دھوم کیتو : اگر یقین نہ آئے تو تجربہ کر لیجئے۔
دمڑی پرشاد : اچھا تو زیادہ سے زیادہ سرمایہ کتنا لگے گا ؟
دھوم کیتو : زیادہ سے زیادہ۔ یہی کوئی پانچ لاکھ۔
دمڑی پرشاد : پانچ لاکھ تو کوئی زیادہ نہیں۔
دھوم کیتو : تو پھر لائیے ہاتھ۔ کہو تو آج ہی مہورت کر دیں۔
دمڑی پرشاد : لیکن سٹوری یعنی کہانی کا کیا ہوگا۔
دھوم کیتو : اس کی فکر نہ کیجئے۔ یہ سب مجھ پر چھوڑ دیجئے۔ میرے ایک دوست ہیں مرزا بوڑم بیگ۔ ایسی کہانی لکھیں گے کہ بدن کے رونگٹے کھڑے ہو جائیں گے۔
دمڑی پرشاد : بوڑم بیگ ! عجیب سا نام ہے۔
دھوم کیتو : نام تو عجیب ہے ہی۔ شکل اس سے بھی زیادہ عجیب ہے بس، یوں سمجھ لیجئے کہ ایک دم نہ صرف بوڑم نظر آتے ہیں بلکہ دراصل ہیں

بھی بوڑم ہی! ہر لحاظ سے بوڑم۔ میرا مطلب ہے کہ جسمانی اور خاندانی لحاظ سے ان کا کوئی نام ہو سکتا ہے تو وہ بوڑم ہے۔

دمڑی پرشاد: اچھا تو کبھی ان سے ملاقات تو کرائیے۔

دھوم کیتو: آج ہی لیجئے۔ میں ابھی ان کو بلوا بھیجتا ہوں۔ پہلی ملاقات ہی میں آپ مان جائیں گے کہ ہماری فلم کی کہانی بوڑم صاحب کے علاوہ کوئی نہیں لکھ سکتا۔

دمڑی پرشاد: اور گانے" کون لکھے گا۔

دھوم کیتو: گانوں کا بھی انتظام ہو جائے گا۔ میرے ایک اور دوست ہیں سرگم شکارپوری۔ بخدا گانے لکھتے ہیں کہ جادو کرتے ہیں۔ بھلا چنگا انسان سُنے تو اس پہ وجد یعنی وحشت طاری ہو جائے۔ بس یوں سمجھ لیجئے کہ ایک ایک گانا ایسا ہوگا کہ سارے ہندوستان میں ایک کہرام مچ جائے گا۔

دمڑی پرشاد: ہیرو اور ہیروئن کے متعلق آپ نے کیا سوچا ہے؟

دھوم کیتو: ہیرو تو کوئی بھی شخص ہو سکتا ہے۔ اس کے متعلق سوچنا بیکار ہے۔ اگر کوئی اور نہ ملا تو خاکسار حاضر ہے۔ ہیروئن کے متعلق عرض ہے کہ ایک لڑکی ہے شنگار بیگم۔ سیٹھ صاحب ذرا نام ملاحظہ فرمائیے۔ شنگار بیگم! میں اسے کبھی جانتا تھا۔ خیر ہٹائیے اسے۔ ع

یہ قصہ ہے جب کا کہ آتش جواں تھا

اب تو صاحب مہینوں ملاقات کی نوبت نہیں آتی۔ میرا خیال ہے کہ

ہیروئن کا پارٹ اسے دیا جائے۔ ایکٹنگ تو وہ بالکل نہیں جانتی لیکن شکل وصورت ایسی پائی ہے کہ آپ دیکھیں گے تو ایک دم اس پر لٹو ہو جائیں گے۔ اور میری رائے میں ہیروئن میں یہی ایک خوبی ہونی چاہیے۔ یعنی آدمی دیکھے تو فوراً . . . . .

دمڑی پرشاد: مجھے آپ سے بالکل اتفاق ہے لیکن وہ لے گی کیا!

دھوم کیتو: لینے دینے کی بات چھوڑیئے۔ اس کے پاس پرماتما کا دیا ہوا سب کچھ ہے۔ وہ تو محض شوق کی خاطر یا یوں کہیئے کہ میری خاطر یا آرٹ کی خاطر یا ہم سب کی خاطر فلم لائن میں آنا چاہتی ہے۔

دمڑی پرشاد: لیکن شنگا ربیگم کوئی اچھا نام نہیں۔ کیا اسے بدلا نہیں جا سکتا

دھوم کیتو: کیوں نہیں۔ کیوں نہیں۔ شنگا ربیگم کی بجائے آپ اسے کجلا یا بگلا۔ ریوا یا میوہ۔ رجنی یا سجنی کوئی بھی نام دے سکتے ہیں میرے خیال میں اسے کوئی بھی عذر نہ ہوگا۔

دمڑی پرشاد: سب سے ضروری بات تو میں نے آپ سے پوچھی ہی نہیں۔

دھوم کیتو: ہاں ہاں فرمائیے۔ ایسی کونسی بات ہے!

دمڑی پرشاد: آپ فلم ڈائرکٹ کرنے کا کیا لیں گے؟

دھوم کیتو: (قہقہہ لگا کر) ہاہاہا۔ بڑی ضروری بات پوچھی آپ نے! بندہ پرور میں تو ڈرہی گیا تھا۔ دیکھیے۔ لینے دینے کے متعلق یہ عرض ہے کہ مجھے کچھ بھی دے دیجیے! لیکن صرف اتنی بات کا خیال رکھئے کہ میری اصلی تنخواہ اور فلیمی تنخواہ میں کافی فرق ہونا چاہیے۔

دمڑی پرشاد: میں آپ کا مطلب نہیں سمجھا۔

دھوم کیتو: دیکھئے سیٹھ صاحب۔ فلم لائن میں ہر شخص کی دو تنخواہیں ہوتی ہیں ایک اصلی۔ دوسری پبلسٹی۔ مثال کے طور پر میری اصل تنخواہ تو ہوگی صرف تین سو روپے۔ لیکن میری پبلسٹی تنخواہ ہوگی تین ہزار۔ سمجھے آپ اس نکتے کو!

دمڑی پرشاد: بالکل۔ بالکل۔ مجھے منظور ہے۔ آپ آج ہی سے فلم کی تیاری شروع کر دیجئے۔

دوسرا منظر

(مرزا بوڑم بیگ کا کمرہ)

(دھوم کیتو اور بوڑم بیگ ایک بینچ پر بیٹھے ہوئے ہیں)

دھوم کیتو: (قہقہہ لگا کر) ہاتھ لاؤ استاد بوڑم۔ ایسی مرغی پھنسی ہے کہ وارے نیارے ہو جائیں گے۔

بوڑم بیگ: لیکن یہ سیٹھ دمڑی پرشاد ہیں کون۔ میں نے تو ان کا نام پہلی بار سنا ہے۔

دھوم کیتو: کیا بتاؤں۔ بس یوں سمجھ لیجئے کہ نرے کاٹھ کے اُلو ہیں۔ بلکہ میرا تو خیال ہے کہ انھیں کاٹھ کا اُلو کہنا بھی بے چارے کاٹھ کے اُلو کی توہین ہے۔

بوڑم بیگ: لیکن وہ آپ کے جال میں پھنس کیسے گئے۔

دھوم کیتو: (ہنس کر) اجی بوڑم صاحب کاٹھ کا اُلّو نہیں پھنسے گا تو کیا ہم تم پھنسیں گے۔ خیر اب آپ جلدی سے ایک کہانی لکھ ڈالئے۔ باقی سب انتظام میں کر لوں گا۔

بوڑم بیگ: کس قسم کی کہانی چاہتے ہیں آپ!

دھوم کیتو: نام ذرا مزے دار ہونا چاہئے۔ جیسے "کلا وناش عرف ستیاناس"۔ پلاٹ ہو چٹ پٹا سا۔ قدم قدم پر محبت منٹ منٹ بعد ایک آدھ بھڑکیلا منظر۔ بس کہانی کیا ہو، کہانی کیا ہو، بارہ مسالے کی چاٹ ہو۔

بوڑم بیگ: آپ تسلی فرمائیے۔ کہانی بالکل ایسی ہی ہوگی کہ ایک بار تو سیٹھ صاحب سُن کر بھڑک اٹھیں گے۔ اگر ہنس ہنس کر پاگل نہ ہو جائیں تو میرا نام بدل دیجئے گا۔

دھوم کیتو: اچھا تو اب میں چلتا ہوں۔ آپ کل دس بجے کہانی لے کر سیٹھ صاحب کے یہاں مجھے ملئے۔ پتہ نوٹ کر لیجئے۔ ۱۲۵ بچری روڈ۔ سرگم شکار پوری کو بھی کہلوا بھیجا ہے۔ وہ بھی گلے لیکر وہاں پہنچ جائے گا۔

تیسرا منظر

سیٹھ دمڑی پرشاد کا کمرہ

(سیٹھ دمڑی پرشاد بہی کھاتہ دیکھ رہے ہیں۔ دھوم کیتو

اور بوڑم بیگ، داخل ہوتے ہیں)

دھوم کیتو: آداب عرض۔ سیٹھ صاحب . . . . مرزا بوڑم بیگ سے ملئے۔ آپ اپنے وقت کے سب سے بڑے سٹوری رائٹر ہیں۔ فلم لائن میں آپ کو مہا لیکھک بوڑم اعظم کے لقب سے یاد کیا جاتا ہے۔ اور آپ ہیں سیٹھ دمڑی پرشاد!

بوڑم بیگ: (مصافحہ کرتے ہوئے) بڑی خوشی ہوئی آپ سے مل کر۔

دمڑی پرشاد: (بوڑم سے) تشریف رکھئے۔ مہا بوڑم اعظم لیکھک صاحب۔

بوڑم بیگ: معاف کیجیے گا۔ میرا نام مہا لیکھک بوڑم اعظم ہے۔

دمڑی پرشاد: اوہ۔ معاف کیجیے گا بوڑم صاحب۔

دھوم کیتو: سیٹھ صاحب! بوڑم اعظم کہئے۔ محض بوڑم نہیں۔

دمڑی پرشاد: اوہ! دوبارہ معاف کیجئے۔

دھوم کیتو: سیٹھ صاحب۔ بوڑم اعظم نے ہماری فلم کے لئے کہانی لکھی ہے۔ کہانی کیا ہے۔ کہانی کیا ہے۔ طمانچہ ہے۔ فلم انڈسٹری کے منہ پر طمانچہ۔ ایسا زبردست طمانچہ کہ فلم انڈسٹری چیخ اٹھے گی۔

دمڑی پرشاد: اوہ! کافی خطرناک کہانی معلوم ہوتی ہے۔

بوڑم بیگ: نہیں نہیں سیٹھ صاحب! آپ تو یونہی گھبرا گئے۔ ذرہ بھر بھی خطرناک نہیں۔ دراصل بات یہ ہے سیٹھ صاحب کہ میں خالص لٹریچر لکھتا ہوں۔ مطلب یہ کہ میں کہانی ایسی لکھتا ہوں جسے لٹریچر کہا جاتا ہے۔ بس یہی مجھ میں خوبی ہے۔ ویسے لکھنے کو کون کہانی نہیں لکھ رہا۔

چمڑے کے سوداگر کہانیاں لکھ رہے ہیں۔ جوتے بیچنے والے کہانیاں لکھ رہے ہیں۔ حتیٰ کہ جوتے چرانے والے بھی کہانیاں لکھ رہے ہیں۔ کہانی لکھنے کا مرض یوں کہیئے کہ وبا کی طرح پھیل رہا ہے۔ لیکن معاف کیجئے میں جو کہانی لکھتا ہوں، وہ خالص لٹریچر ہوتا ہے۔

دمڑی پرشاد: یہ لٹریچر کیا بلا ہوتا ہے۔

بوڑم بیگ: لٹریچر یعنی لٹریچر کو کہتے ہیں۔ جو بالکل۔ جو یعنی۔ جو سو فیصدی...

دھوم کیتو: ہاں ہاں جو سو فیصدی لٹریچر ہو۔ یعنی جسے ایک بچہ بھی پڑھے تو فوراً پکار اُٹھے کہ یہ لٹریچر ہے۔

دمڑی پرشاد: خیر ہوتا ہوگا۔ اچھا تو کیا آپ اس کہانی کا خلاصہ سُنا سکتے ہیں؟

بوڑم بیگ: اسی لئے تو حاضر ہوا ہوں۔ ملاحظہ فرمایئے۔ کہانی کا نام میں نے ڈائرکٹر صاحب کی اجازت سے رکھا ہے "کلا وناش عرف ستیاناس"

پہلے تو یہ کہیئے کہ نام پسند آیا؟

دمڑی پرشاد: کافی اچھا نام ہے۔

بوڑم بیگ: شکریہ۔ مجھے معلوم تھا کہ نام ضرور پسند آئے گا۔ کہانی بھی ضرور پسند آئے گی۔

دمڑی پرشاد: پہلے ذرا سُنا تو دیجئے کہ کہانی کس قسم کی ہے۔

بوڑم بیگ: کہانی کی کچھ نہ پوچھئے۔ بس یہ سمجھ لیجئے کہ.... کہ۔

دھوم کیتو: کہ سو فیصدی لٹریچر ہے۔

دمڑی پرشاد: مجھے کہانی سنائیے۔ لٹریچر۔ وٹ ریچر رہنے دیجئے۔

بوڑم بیگ : بہت اچھا۔ تو سُنئے۔ کہانی کا ہیرو پریم کمار جو پریم نگر کا رہنے والا ہے۔ اپنے ہمسائے پریم ناتھ کی نوجوان لڑکی پریم کماری سے پریم کرتا ہے۔

دھوم کیتو : کیا کہنے۔ کیا کہنے بوڑم صاحب۔ کیا بات پیدا کی ہے۔

بوڑم بیگ : آداب عرض.... ہاں صاحب۔ تو پریم کمار پریم کماری سے پریم کرتا ہے۔ لیکن وہ اس انداز سے پریم کرتا ہے کہ کسی کو پتہ نہیں چلنے دیتا کہ آیا وہ پریم کر رہا ہے یا پاگل خانے جانے کی تیاری۔ کبھی اپنی محبوبہ کو دیکھ کر ہنسنے لگتا ہے کبھی رونے لگتا ہے کبھی داڑھی بڑھا لیتا ہے کبھی مونچھیں کٹوا دیتا ہے۔ کبھی سرد سرد آہیں بھرتا ہے اور کبھی گرم گرم پکوڑے کھاتا ہے۔

دمڑی پرشاد : کیا کہنے۔ کیا کہنے۔ واقعی محبت کا یہ انداز بہت نرالا ہے۔

بوڑم بیگ : ابھی کیا سُنا ہے۔ آپ نے۔ ذرا آگے چل کر دیکھئے۔ کیا کیا گُل کھلتے ہیں۔ جی ہاں۔ تو صاحب پہلا گل یہ کھلتا ہے کہ پریم کماری کی ماں کو اس چوری چھپے کی محبت کا علم ہو جاتا ہے اور وہ پریم کماری کو مار مار کر ـــ مار مار کر اس کا بھرکس نکال دیتی ہے۔

دمڑی پرشاد : بہت خوب۔ ایسی لڑکیوں کے ساتھ ایسا ہی سلوک ہونا چاہیے۔

بوڑم بیگ : جی ہاں۔ دراصل اس سین کا مطلب یہ ہے کہ نوجوان لڑکیوں کو عبرت حاصل کرنی چاہیئے۔ یعنی انھیں چھپ چھپ کر اپنے ہمسائے کے لڑکے سے محبت نہیں کرنی چاہیئے۔

دمڑی پرشاد: کھلم کھلا محبت کے متعلق آپ کی کیا رائے ہے!

بوڑم بیگ: یہ میں پھر کبھی آپ کو بتاؤں گا۔ کیونکہ کھلم کھلا محبت کا اپنی کہانی سے کوئی تعلق نہیں۔ ہاں صاحب تو پریم کماری کو ایک کمرے میں بند کر دیا جاتا ہے۔ اور یہاں پریم کمار اور پریم کماری مل کر ایک دوگانا گاتے ہیں۔

دمڑی پرشاد: لیکن پریم کمار بند کمرے میں کیسے آگیا؟

دھوم کیتو: سیٹھ صاحب اسے سمجھنا آپ کے بس کا روگ نہیں۔ یہ ٹیکنیکل پوائنٹ ہے۔ کئی لوگ اسے کیمرا ٹرک (CAMERA TRICK) بھی کہتے ہیں۔ خیر آپ کی جانے بلا۔ بس آپ فرض کر لیجئے کہ پریم کمار بند کمرے میں آجاتا ہے۔ ورنہ دوگانے کا ..... ورنہ دوگانے کا۔

سرگم شکارپوری: (کمرے میں داخل ہوتے ہوئے) ورنہ دو.... دو... گانے کا ستیاناس ہو جائیگا۔

دمڑی پرشاد: (سرگم کی طرف دیکھتے ہوئے) آپ کون ہیں؟

دھوم کیتو: اوہ! آپ ہیں سرگم شکارپوری۔ اپنے دور کے سب سے بڑے شاعر۔ مہاکوی۔ شاعرِ اعظم۔ سرگم شکارپوری صاحب۔

دمڑی پرشاد: (سرگم کی طرف غور سے دیکھنے کے بعد) آپ تو مجسم ادھو نیم نظر آتے ہیں۔

سرگم شکارپوری: شُک شُک۔ شُک۔ شکریہ۔ شکریہ۔ دراصل میرا نام پن پن پنڈت رونقی رام رونق ہے۔ لیکن میرے سب دو... دو۔

دوست مجھے سرگم ش شکار پوری کہتے ہیں۔ یہاں تک کہ میری بی۔ بی۔۔بی۔۔۔۔ بیوی بھی سرگم ڈا۔۔۔ ڈا۔۔۔۔ ڈارلنگ کہنے لگی ہے۔

دھوم کیتو: سرگم صاحب ہمیں اپنی فلم کے لئے ایک مزیدار دوگانے کی ضرورت ہے۔ کیا آپ کے پاس کوئی ایسا دوگانا ہے!

سرگم شکار پوری: اجی صاحب۔ دو۔ دو۔۔۔۔ دوگانے تو مجھ سے تھو۔تھو تھوک کے بھاؤ لے لیجئے۔ جو۔ جو۔ جوتا پہنتے پہنتے دوگانا لکھ ڈالتا ہوں۔"

دھوم کیتو: سچوایشن (SITUATION) اچھی طرح سمجھ لیجئے۔ ہیروئن کو اس کی ماں نے بیدردی سے پیٹا ہے۔ وہ ایک کمرے میں بند کر دی گئی ہے۔ جہاں ہیرو صاحب چاندنی رات میں اس سے ملتے ہیں اور ملنے سے پیشتر دوگانے کا پہلا بول گاتے ہیں۔

سرگم شکار پوری۔ سچ۔ سچ۔ سچ۔ سچوایشن میں نے بالکل سمجھ لی ہے۔ دراصل مے۔مے۔ میرا واسطہ اس قسم کی سچ۔ سچ۔ سچ۔ سچوایشنز سے ہی اکثر رہتا ہے۔ یہ دیکھئے۔ میں نے فل۔ فل۔ فلمی گانوں کی چھ فائلیں تیار کر رکھی ہیں۔ پہلی فائل کا نام ہے پ۔پ۔پ پریم کے گانے۔ ان گانوں میں پریم ہی پریم ہے۔ دوسری فائل ہے۔مو۔مو موت کے گانے۔ ان گانوں میں موت ہی موت ہے۔ تیسری فائل شا۔شا۔ شادی کے گانے اور چوتھی بر بر بربادی کے گانے۔ پانچویں میں ہیں ق ق ق۔ قوالیاں۔ اور چھٹی ابھی خا خا خالی پڑی ہے۔

دھوم کیتو: بہت خوب۔ بہت خوب۔ اچھا کوئی مزیدار دوگانا سیٹھ صاحب کو ذرا ترنم کے ساتھ سنائیے۔

سرگم شکارپوری: سنئے صاحب

جگ جگ جگمگاتی رات میرا چندا میرے ساتھ
اماں سو رہی ہے
جھل جھل جھلملاتی رات میری گھڑی بجائے سات
منّی رو رہی ہے

دھڑی پرشاد: معاف کیجیے گا سرگم صاحب۔ لیکن منّی کے رونے کا اس دوگانے سے کیا تعلق ہے!

سرگم شکارپوری: وا۔ وا۔ سیٹھ صاحب۔ آپ یہ بھی نہیں سمجھ پائے۔ بن بن۔ بن بندہ پرور! اس دوگانے میں، میں نے چاند۔ چاند۔ چاندنی رات کا نقشہ پیش کیا ہے۔ آپ جانتے ہیں کہ جب ام۔ ام۔ اماں سوتی ہے تو منّی رویا کرتی ہے۔ دوسرے بچے سا۔ سات بجے کے قریب ضرور روتے ہیں۔ کیونکہ اس وقت انھیں بھو بھو بھوک لگتی ہے۔

دھوم کیتو: واہ سرگم صاحب۔ واہ! واہ! کیا نکتہ پیدا کیا ہے۔

سرگم شکارپوری: آداب عرض۔ کہیئے دوگانا پسند آیا؟

دھوم کیتو: اچھا ہے۔ کافی اچھا ہے۔ ایک آدھ اور سنا دیجئے۔

سرگم شکارپوری: سنیئے۔ عرض کیا ہے:۔

ٹن ٹن ٹن ۔ میرا بھو ۔ بھو ۔ بھولا سجن
ہائے میں کیا کروں ۔ ہائے میں کیا کروں
چھن چھن چھن میری بھولی دلہن
کہیں ڈوب مروں ۔ کہیں ڈوب مروں
ٹم ۔ ٹم ۔ ٹم ۔ میرا بھولا بلم
میں تو آہیں بھروں ۔ ہائے آہیں بھروں
چھم ۔ چھم ۔ چھم ۔ مجھے کھائے یہی غم
کیسے پیار کروں ۔ ہائے پیار کروں

دھوم کیتو : بہت خوب سرگم صاحب ۔ آپ نے تو قلم توڑ کر رکھ دیا ہے۔
سرگم تشکار پوری : اجی تو ۔ تو ۔ توڑا کہاں ہے ۔ وہ کم کم کم بخت تو ابھی میری جیب میں سلامت پڑا ہے ۔
دمڑی پرشاد : سرگم صاحب ۔ آپ کی جتنی تعریف کی جائے کم ہے ۔ دوگانا لکھنے میں تو آپ کو کمال حاصل ہے ۔
سرگم تشکار پوری : بن بن بن بندہ نوازی ہے ۔ ورنہ خاخا خاکسار کس قابل ہے ۔
دھوم کیتو : ہاں تو سیٹھ صاحب باقی کہانی بھی سن لیجیے ۔ بوڑم صاحب انتظار کر رہے ہیں ۔
دمڑی پرشاد : ہاں بوڑم صاحب ۔ باقی کہانی بھی سنا دیجیے ۔

بوڑم بیگ: ہاں صاحب تو پریم کماری کو جب کمرے میں بند کیا جاتا ہے اور پریم کمار اس سے ملاقات کرنے کے بعد گھر جاتا ہے۔ تو سین اس وقت کہیں قریب سے گھڑی بارہ بجاتی ہے اور دُور سے اُلّو کی چیخ سنائی دیتی ہے۔ اُلّو کی چیخ سن کر پریم کماری بے ہوش ہو جاتی ہے۔

دھوم کیتو: کیا کہنے کیا کہنے۔ یہ بالکل نیا ٹچ ہے۔ کم از کم میں نے کسی فلم میں نہیں دیکھا کہ اُلّو کی چیخ سن کر ہیروئن بے ہوش ہو جائے۔

بوڑم بیگ: جی ہاں۔ یہ بالکل انوکھا ٹچ ہے۔ تو صاحب! جب صبح پریم کماری کی ماں دروازہ کھولتی ہے تو کیا دیکھتی ہے۔ کیا دیکھتی ہے کہ پریم کماری غائب ہے اور اس کی بجائے بستر پر ایک بہت بڑا سا اُلّو سو رہا ہے۔

دمڑی پرشاد: (حیرانی سے) ہائیں! لڑکی کی بجائے اُلّو؟

بوڑم بیگ: جی ہاں اُلّو! بالکل اُلّو! یعنی ایک دم اُلّو! اس ٹچ سے میں نے SUSPENSE پیدا کرنے کی کوشش کی ہے۔

دھوم کیتو: اور حق تو یہ ہے کہ خوب SUSPENSE پیدا کی ہے۔

بوڑم بیگ: اُلّو کو دیکھ کر پریم کماری کی ماں بے ہوش ہو جاتی ہے اسے ہسپتال میں پہنچایا جاتا ہے۔ جہاں ہوش میں آنے کے بعد وہ ایک، کمپونڈر سے محبت کرنے لگتی ہے۔

دمڑی پرشاد: شادی شدہ عورت کمپونڈر سے محبت کرنے لگتی ہے یہ آپ کیا کہہ رہے ہیں؟

بوڑم بیگ: سیٹھ صاحب۔ شاید میں نے آپ کو نہیں بتایا کہ پریم کماری کی ماں بیوہ ہے۔ دراصل میں اس کہانی میں ایک بڑے نازک سماجی مسئلے کا حل پیش کرنا چاہتا ہوں میری مراد ودھوا دواہ سے ہے۔

دمڑی پرشاد: ہاں تو اس کے بعد کیا ہوتا ہے!

بوڑم بیگ: اس کے بعد ایک عجیب واقعہ پیش آتا ہے۔ پریم کمار پریم کماری کی کھوج میں گھر سے نکلتا ہے۔ شہر سے دور ایک شمشان کے قریب اس کی ملاقات ایک بدصورت عورت سے ہوتی ہے جسے دیکھ کر پریم کمار بے ہوش ہو جاتا ہے۔ اسے ہسپتال لے جایا جاتا ہے جہاں ہوش میں آنے کے بعد وہ پریم کماری کی ماں سے جو کہ اس ہسپتال میں اب نرس بنی ہوئی ہے لڑنے لگتا ہے۔

دمڑی پرشاد: اس کے بعد؟

بوڑم بیگ: اس کے بعد وہ ایک بار پھر پریم کماری کی تلاش میں روانہ ہوتا ہے۔ ایک شہر سے دوسرے شہر۔ ایک گاؤں سے دوسرے گاؤں۔ ہر راہ گیر کو روک کر پوچھتا ہے۔ کیا تم نے پریم کماری کو دیکھا ہے؟ کیا تم پریم کماری کو جانتے ہو؟ کیا تم مجھے پریم کماری کے پاس لے چلو گے؟

دھوم کیتو: بہت خوب۔ بہت خوب۔ یہ واقعی بڑا ڈرامیٹک ٹچ ہے۔

بوڑم بیگ: جی ہاں۔ پریم کمار یہ سوال اتنی بار کرتا ہے کہ اس کا گلا بیٹھ جاتا ہے۔ وہ ایک بار پھر ہسپتال میں جاتا ہے اور اپنے گلے میں دوا لگوا کر

پریم کماری کی ماں کے نئے خاوند سے ہاتھا پائی کرنے لگتا ہے۔ دونوں گتھم گتھا ہو جاتے ہیں۔ اس لڑائی میں ہسپتال کی شیشیاں، میزیں کرسیاں توڑی جاتی ہیں۔ آخر ہسپتال کا بڑا ڈاکٹر بیچ بچاؤ کر کے دونوں کی صلح کرا دیتا ہے۔

دمڑی پرشاد: پھر کیا ہوتا ہے؟

بوڑم بیگ: ہسپتال سے آنے کے بعد پریم کمار بالکل مایوس ہو جاتا ہے اور خودکشی کرنے کے ارادے سے قطب مینار پر چڑھنے لگتا ہے۔

دھوم کیتو: میرے خیال میں آج تک کسی فلم میں قطب مینار سے کود کر خودکشی کرنے کا منظر نہیں دکھایا گیا۔

بوڑم بیگ: جی ہاں۔ آپ کا خیال بالکل صحیح ہے۔ ہاں صاحب تو جب پریم کمار قطب مینار کی آخری منزل پر پہنچتا ہے تو کیا دیکھتا ہے کہ ایک نوجوان اس سے پہلے خودکشی کرنے کی غرض سے کھڑا ہے۔ یہ نوجوان دراصل پریم کماری ہے۔

سرگم شکارپوری: پ۔ پ۔ پپ۔ پریم کماری ہے۔ واہ۔واہ۔ بو بو بوڑم صاحب کیا بات ہے۔

بوڑم بیگ: جی ہاں پریم کماری ایک لڑکے کے بھیس میں وہاں کھڑی ہے آنکھوں سے آنکھیں چار ہوتی ہیں۔ دونوں ایک دوسرے کو پہچان لیتے ہیں۔ اور وہیں کھڑے کھڑے ایک دوگانہ گاتے ہیں۔

دمڑی پرشاد: بہت خوب۔ لیکن آپ نے یہ نہیں بتایا کہ گھر سے غائب

ہونے کے بعد پریم کماری کہاں جاتی ہے۔

بوڑم بیگ: سیٹھ صاحب ابھی تو اس کہانی کی سب سے بڑی خوبی ہے۔ فلم دیکھنے والے سوچ سوچ کر پاگل ہو جائیں گے کہ پریم کماری کہاں گئی۔ لیکن انھیں کچھ پتہ نہیں چلے گا۔ اس بچ سے تو میں نے زبردست SUSPENSE پیدا کرنے کی کوشش کی ہے۔ کیوں ڈائرکٹر صاحب۔ کیا خیال ہے آپ کا؟

دھوم کیتو: بوڑم صاحب۔ آپ بجا فرماتے ہیں۔ دراصل جب تک کہ کہانی میں SUSPENSE نہ ہو وہ بالکل بیکار ہے اور آپ کی کہانی میں تو SUSPENSE اس قدر ہے۔ اس قدر ہے کہ معلوم ہوتا ہے کہ اس میں SUSPENSE کے علاوہ اور کچھ ہے ہی نہیں۔

بوڑم بیگ: آداب عرض۔ آداب عرض۔

دمڑی پرشاد: میرے خیال میں کہانی میں کافی جان ہے۔

بوڑم بیگ: اجی صاحب۔ جان کیسے نہ ہو گی۔ اس میں پندرہ CLIMAX ہیں۔ ۳۶۔ ACCIDENTS ہیں۔ اور چالیس گانوں کی گنجائش ہے۔ اور پھر سب سے بڑی خوبی یہ کہ اک دم کامیڈی۔ شروع سے آخر تک COMEDY یعنی ہنستے ہنستے پیٹ میں بل پڑ جائیں گے۔ گولڈن نہیں تو سلور جوبلی تو ضرور منائے گی۔

سرگم شکارپوری: ہاں ہاں صاحب کیوں نہیں منائے گی۔ آپ کی دعا سے ایک ایک گانا ایسا ہوگا کہ ہٹ سانگ، ہر کوچوان۔ ہر ٹیکسی ڈرائیور

ہر نتھا نتھو خیرا اسے گاتا نہ پھرے تو سرگم نام نہیں۔

دھوم کیتو: اور ڈائرکشن ایسی ہوگی سیٹھ صاحب کہ لوگ دانتوں تلے انگلیاں دبائے پھریں گے۔ آپ کی دعا سے ایسے ایسے ٹچ ہوں گے کہ ہالی ووڈ سے چل کر لوگ اسے دیکھنے آئیں گے۔

دمڑی پرشاد: اگر یہ بات ہے تو آپ پرماتما کا نام لے کر شوٹنگ شروع کر دیجیے۔ روپے کی پروا نہ کیجیے۔ پانی کی طرح بہائیے۔ لیکن ایک دفعہ فلم ایسی بنا دیجیے کہ چوگنے نہیں تو کم از کم تگنے تو ضرور ہو جائیں۔

دھوم کیتو: آپ تسلی رکھیے سیٹھ صاحب.... ہاں کوئی اور بات؟

دمڑی پرشاد: اور تو کوئی خاص بات نہیں۔ ہاں... آپ نے ابھی شنگار بیگم سے ملاقات نہیں کرائی۔

دھوم کیتو: اوہ۔ شنگار بیگم۔ میں نے اسے کہہ دیا ہے۔ دو ایک دن میں وہ آپ سے ملنے کے لئے آئے گی۔

دمڑی پرشاد: اچھا تو اب آپ لوگ جا سکتے ہیں۔

دھوم کیتو۔ بوڑم بیگ۔ سرگم شنکار پوری: آداب عرض!

چوتھا منظر

دھوم کیتو کا کمرا

(دھوم کیتو گھنٹی بجاتا ہے۔ چپڑاسی اندر آتا ہے)

دھوم کیتو: (چپڑاسی سے) دیکھو۔ ہم نے کچھ ٹھیک مکالمے لکھنے کے لئے

بلائے ہیں۔ انھیں باری باری اندر بھیجدو۔

چپڑاسی : بہت اچھا سرکار۔

(ایک لیکھک اندر آتا ہے)

لیکھک : آداب عرض۔

دھوم کیتو: آداب عرض

لیکھک : کیا میں بیٹھ سکتا ہوں۔

دھوم کیتو: نہیں آپ کھڑے ہی رہیں تو بہتر ہوگا۔ آپ کا نام؟

لیکھک : نوین چندر۔

دھوم کیتو: تعلیم؟

لیکھک : ایم۔اے۔ ایل۔ ایل۔ بی۔ پی۔ ایچ۔ ڈی

دھوم کیتو: آپ سے کس مسخرے نے کہا کہ آپ مکالمے لکھا کریں۔

لیکھک : کیوں صاحب۔ مجھ میں کیا نقص نظر آیا آپ کو۔ میں چھ کتابوں کا مُصنّف ہوں۔ کافی تعلیم یافتہ ہوں۔ میں مکالمے کیوں نہیں لکھ سکتا؟

دھوم کیتو: برخوردار! فلمی مکالمے لکھنے کے لئے تعلیم کی ضرورت ہے نہ لیاقت کی۔ اس کے لئے ضرورت ہے لاعلمی اور ناواقفیت کی۔ یعنی جسے ہم دوسرے لفظوں میں فلمی تجربہ کہہ سکتے ہیں۔ اس لئے آپ تشریف لے جائیں۔

(چپڑاسی سے) دوسرے امیدوار کو بلاؤ۔

چپڑاسی: بہت اچھا سرکار۔

(دوسرا امیدوار داخل ہوتاہے)

دوسرا امیدوار: نمستے ڈائرکٹر صاحب۔

دھوم کیتو: نمستے۔ آپ کی تعلیم؟

دوسرا امیدوار: مڈل فیل ہوں۔

دھوم کیتو: بہت خوب۔ تجربہ؟

دوسرا امیدوار: میں نے دس فلموں کے مکالمے لکھے ہیں۔

دھوم کیتو: ان فلموں کے نام بتائیے۔

دوسرا امیدوار: ان فلموں کے نام ہیں "ابابیل"۔ "لکڑ بگڑ"۔ "خونی چھپیا"۔ "شمشان" "قبرستان کا بھوت"۔ "شریر بندر"۔ "کالا چور"۔ "بھورا ہاتھی"۔ "وغیرہ وغیرہ۔

دھوم کیتو: اچھا فلم "وغیرہ وغیرہ" کے مکالموں کا ایک نمونہ سنائیے۔

دوسرا امیدوار: ملاحظہ فرمائیے۔ رمیش اس فلم کا ہیرو ہے۔ اور نیلما ہیروئن۔
رمیش نیلما سے کہتا ہے۔ "نیلما۔ نیلما۔ او نیلما۔ جب تم مجھے نظر نہیں آتیں تو مجھے ایسا معلوم ہوتا ہے، جیسے میں اندھا ہو گیا ہوں۔ جیسے ساری دنیا میں اندھیرا چھا گیا ہے۔ اور سورج ہمیشہ ہمیشہ کے لئے غروب ہو گیا ہے"

دھوم کیتو: کیا کہنے۔ کیا کہنے۔ اور نیلما کیا کہتی ہے؟

دوسرا امیدوار: نیلما کہتی ہے۔ "رمیش اور جو میری حالت ہوتی ہے۔ کاش وہ میں بیان کر سکتی۔ بس یوں محسوس ہوتا ہے۔ جیسے کہ میں ایک دم پاگل ہو گئی ہوں۔ جیسے میری روح کے ویرانے میں اُلّو بول رہے ہیں۔ چمگادڑیں چکر لگا رہی ہیں اور مرغ اذانیں دے رہے ہیں۔

دھوم کیتو: خوب بہت خوب۔ مرغ اذانیں دے رہے ہیں کا واقعی جواب

نہیں۔ بخدا۔ کیا فقرہ لکھ گئے ہیں آپ۔

دوسرا امیدوار: آپ کی عنایت ہے ورنہ میں.....

دھوم کیتو: آپ یہ کہانی لے جائیے۔ اور اس کے مکالمے لکھ ڈالئے۔

دوسرا امیدوار: معاوضہ کیا ملے گا!

دھوم کیتو: مکمل مکالمے لکھنے کے آپ کو تین سو روپے ملیں گے۔ اس میں سے سو روپیہ میری کمیشن ہوگی۔ دس روپے پیشگی لے جائیے۔ اور باقی کام ختم ہونے پر۔

دوسرا امیدوار: یہ تو بہت تھوڑا ہے۔

دھوم کیتو: تھوڑا! معلوم ہوتا ہے آپ بڑے لالچی ہیں۔ آپ کو معلوم ہے کہ فلم "پان کا بیڑہ" کے مکمل مکالمے میں نے بچاسی روپے میں لکھوائے تھے اور اینٹ کی بیگم کے صرف پچھتر روپے میں۔

دوسرا امیدوار: کچھ بڑھا دیجئے۔

دھوم کیتو: ایک پائی نہیں۔

دوسرا امیدوار: جی۔ غریب آدمی ہوں۔

دھوم کیتو: ارے میاں۔ دنیا میں کون غریب نہیں۔ ہم کون سے لکھ پتی ہیں۔ اچھا منظور ہیں تین سو روپے۔

دوسرا امیدوار: جی ___ مگر ___ لیکن۔

دھوم کیتو: لیکن ویکن کچھ نہیں۔ منظور ہیں تو کہئے نہیں تو.....

دوسرا امیدوار: جی مجھے منظور ہیں۔

دھوم کیتو: یہ لیجیے کہانی . . . .

(چپڑاسی سے) چپڑاسی۔ باقی لیکھکوں سے کہہ دو کہ وہ جا سکتے ہیں۔

چپڑاسی: بہت اچھا سرکار۔

پانچواں منظر

(سیٹھ دمڑی پرشاد کا کمرہ)

شنگار بیگم: میں اندر آ سکتی ہوں۔

دمڑی پرشاد: کون؟ اوہ! ہاں ہاں تشریف لائیے۔

شنگار بیگم: آداب عرض۔

دمڑی پرشاد: آداب عرض۔ آپ کی تعریف؟

شنگار بیگم: میں ہوں شنگار بیگم یعنی کملا یا گملا یا ریوا یا میوہ یا جو کچھ بھی آپ مجھے کہنا چاہیں۔

دمڑی پرشاد: اوہ! آپ ہماری فلم کی ہیروئن ہیں۔

شنگار بیگم: جی ہاں۔ جی ہاں۔

دمڑی پرشاد: بہت خوشی ہوئی آپ سے مل کر۔ واقعی آپ شنگار بیگم ہیں۔ بلکہ آپ کو تو شنگار بکس کہنا چاہیے۔

شنگار بیگم: شکریہ۔

دمڑی پرشاد: آپ کی عمر کیا ہوگی بھلا؟

شنگار بیگم: پچھلے دس برس سے میری عمر میں سال چلی آ رہی ہے۔ ویسے

لگتی ہیں اٹھارہ برس کی ہوں۔

دمڑی پرشاد: اس میں کیا شک ہے۔ بلکہ مجھے تو یوں محسوس ہوتا ہے، کہ آپ ابھی دودھ پیتی بچی ہیں۔

شنگار بیگم: آپ کے علاوہ ڈائرکٹر صاحب کا بھی یہی خیال ہے۔

دمڑی پرشاد: آپ کیسے تشریف لائیں؟

شنگار بیگم: آپ کی کشش کھینچ لائی۔

دمڑی پرشاد: (توند پر ہاتھ پھیرتے ہوئے) ہماری کشش، (قہقہہ لگا کر) ہاہاہا۔ تو گویا ہم میں بھی کوئی ایسی چیز ہے جو لوگوں کو ہماری طرف کھینچتی ہے۔

شنگار بیگم: ہاں صاحب اس میں کیا شک ہے۔

دمڑی پرشاد: اچھا چائے پیجیے گا یا شربت؟

شنگار بیگم: جی میں صرف سگرٹ پیوں گی۔

دمڑی پرشاد: (بیڑی پیش کرتے ہوئے) لیجیے یہ بیڑی حاضر ہے شوق فرمائیے۔

شنگار بیگم: جی معاف کیجیے۔ میں بیڑی نہیں پیتی۔

دمڑی پرشاد: کوئی بات نہیں۔ آئندہ جب آپ تشریف لائیں گی، سگرٹ کا انتظام کر دیا جائے گا۔

شنگار بیگم: شکریہ۔

دمڑی پرشاد: اچھا آپ رہنے والی کہاں کی ہیں۔ اور فلم لائن میں

کب سے ہیں ؟

شنگار بیگم : جی میں لکھنؤ کی رہنے والی ہوں۔ گانا بجانا الہ آباد میں ہی سیکھا۔ ناچنا بمبئی میں۔ کار چلانا کلکتے میں اور تیرنا رنگون میں۔

دمڑی پرشاد : اوہ۔ تو آپ نے تو گھاٹ گھاٹ کا پانی پیا ہے۔ کافی تجربہ کار ہیں۔

شنگار بیگم : سب آپ کی عنایت ہے۔

دمڑی پرشاد : اچھا تو پھر ایک آدھ گانا ہو جائے۔

شنگار بیگم : معاف کیجئے اس وقت گانے کا موڈ نہیں۔ پھر کبھی سناؤں گی اچھا اب اجازت دیجئے۔

دمڑی پرشاد : اجازت دینے کو تو جی نہیں چاہتا لیکن خیر۔ اب آپ جاسکتی ہیں۔

شنگار بیگم : جانے سے پہلے ایک بات پوچھ سکتی ہوں۔

دمڑی پرشاد : ہاں ہاں بڑے شوق سے۔

شنگار بیگم : کیا میں آپ کو اچھی لگتی ہوں ؟

دمڑی پرشاد : ہاں ہاں۔ کیوں نہیں۔ کیوں نہیں۔

شنگار بیگم : کیا میں خوبصورت ہوں۔

دمڑی پرشاد : کیوں نہیں۔ کیوں نہیں۔ کم از کم میری سیٹھانی سے تو زیادہ خوبصورت ہو۔

شنگار بیگم : شکریہ۔ آداب عرض۔

دمڑی پرشاد: آداب عرض۔ کبھی کبھی ضرور ملا کیجئے۔
شنگار بیگم: (مسکرا کر) کبھی کبھی نہیں ہر روز۔
دمڑی پرشاد: (قہقہہ لگا کر) ہاں ہاں۔ یہ ٹھیک ہے۔ ہر روز۔ ہر روز

چھٹا منظر

(دھوم کیتو کا دفتر)

(دھوم کیتو کے دائیں طرف گھسیٹا رام یعنی ہیرو اور بائیں طرف شنگار بیگم یعنی ہیروئن بیٹھے ہوئے ہیں۔ میز پر شربت بنفشہ کی بوتل اور تین گلاس رکھے ہوئے ہیں۔ گھسیٹا رام کے بال بڑھے ہوئے ہیں۔ لباس میلا۔ حلیہ عجیب و غریب۔ شنگار بیگم کا لباس بھڑکیلا)

دھوم کیتو: (شربت کا گلاس اٹھاتے ہوئے) شربت بنفشہ زکام کے لئے تو اکسیر ہے۔

شنگار بیگم: ایک دم اکسیر ہے۔ ادھر حلق سے نیچے اترا اور ادھر زکام بالکل غائب۔

گھسیٹا رام: کئی بار تو پنسلین سے بھی تیز ثابت ہوتا ہے۔

دھوم کیتو: آپ شاید نہیں جانتے کہ پنسلین بھی بنفشے کے پھولوں سے تیار کی جاتی ہے۔

گھسیٹا رام: جی اچھی طرح جانتا ہوں۔ میرے ایک ماموں مویشیوں کے

ہسپتال میں چپڑاسی ہیں۔ انھوں نے بتایا کہ بنفشے کے پھولوں کے علاوہ دھتورے سے بھی پنسلین تیار کی جا رہی ہے۔

شنگار بیگم: (ہنس کر) ہی ہی ہی۔ دھتورے سے۔ دھتورا تو بہت زہریلا ہوتا ہے۔

گھسیٹا رام: پنسلین بھی کم زہریلی نہیں ہوتی۔ میرے ماموں کا کہنا ہے کہ اگر ایک بھینس کو چھ اونس پینسلین پلا دی جائے تو وہ تڑپ تڑپ کر مر جائے گی۔ کیوں ڈائرکٹر صاحب کیا خیال ہے آپ کا۔

دھوم کیتو: ارے بھئی میں ڈائرکٹر ہوں۔ ڈاکٹر نہیں۔ اچھا۔ چھوڑیئے یہ قصہ۔ اب ذرا کام کی باتیں کریں۔ آپ کو معلوم ہے میں نے آپ کو کس لئے بلایا ہے۔

شنگار بیگم: شربت بنفشہ پینے کے لئے۔

دھوم کیتو: بالکل غلط۔ میں نے آپ کو اس لئے تکلیف دی ہے کہ آپ کو کچھ ہدائتیں دینا چاہتا ہوں۔

گھسیٹا رام۔شنگار بیگم: فرمایئے۔ فرمایئے۔

دھوم کیتو: (گھسیٹا رام سے) پہلی ہدایت آپ کو دی جاتی ہے کہ آپ اپنا حلیہ ذرا بہتر بنانے کی کوشش کریں۔ آپ نے بال بُری طرح سے بڑھا رکھے ہیں۔ ہمت کرکے آج انہیں ترشوا لیجئے۔ اور ہاں یہ میلی بُش شرٹ بھی بدل لیجئے۔ اگر آپ کے پاس صرف ایک بش شرٹ ہے تو اسے ڈبل ریٹ پر دھلوا لیجئے۔ اور ہاں گھسیٹا سگرٹ پینا

چھوڑ دیجئے۔ آپ ہماری فلم کے ہیرو ہیں۔ ہیرو کو گھٹیا۔۔۔۔

گھسیٹا رام: جی میں آپ کی ہدایت بالکل سمجھ گیا۔

دھوم کیتو: (شنگار بیگم سے) اور آپ بھڑکیلے کپڑے پہننا چھوڑ دیئے۔ اگر بال بنانے کا ڈھنگ نہیں آتا تو کسی سے سیکھنے کی کوشش کیجئے اور میک اپ کرتے وقت خیال رکھئے کہ کچھ پاؤڈر ڈبے میں باقی رہ جائے۔ سارا آپ کے چہرے کی نذر نہ ہو جائے۔ سمجھیں آپ۔

شنگار بیگم: جی ہاں۔ بالکل سمجھ گئی۔

دھوم کیتو: اچھا آیئے۔ آج مکالمے کے ایک ٹکڑے کی ریہرسل کر لیں تاکہ سیٹ پر آسانی رہے۔ پہلے میں آپ کو پڑھ کر سناؤں گا۔ اس کے بعد آپ اسے ادا کرنے کی کوشش کیجئے۔ (فائیل سے مکالمہ نکالکر پڑھتا ہے)

"دنیا بہت ظالم ہے پریم۔ یہ دو دلوں کو ملنے نہیں دیتی۔ جب پریمی ایک دوسرے سے پریم کرتے ہیں تو دنیا کے سینے پر سانپ لوٹنے لگتے ہیں۔ ماتھے پر بل پڑ جاتے ہیں۔ آنکھوں میں خون اتر آتا ہے:

(گھسیٹا رام سے) اچھا اب آپ کہیئے۔

گھسیٹا رام: دنیا بڑی جالم ہے شنگار بیگم۔

دھوم کیتو: جالم نہیں، ظالم

گھسیٹا رام: جالم۔ جالم

دھوم کیتو: اے کمبخت ظالم۔

گھسیٹا رام: ہاں ہاں جالم ہی تو کہہ رہا ہوں۔

دھوم کیتو: عجیب آدمی ہو۔ ظالم نہیں کہہ سکتے ۔۔۔۔۔ اچھا۔۔۔۔ یہ لفظ بدل دیا جائے گا اور ہاں شنگار بیگم مت کہو۔ فلم میں شنگار بیگم کا نام پریم کماری ہے۔ جیسے تمہارا نام گھسیٹا رام نہیں پریم کمار ہے۔ اچھا اب باقی فقرے بولو۔

گھسیٹا رام: یہ دو دِلوں کو کبھی ملنے نہیں دیتی۔ جب پریمی ایک دوسرے سے پریم کرتے ہیں تو اس کے سانپوں پر سینے لوٹنے لگتے ہیں۔ ہاتھے پہ بل پڑ جاتے ہیں اور خون میں آنکھیں اتر جاتی ہیں۔

دھوم کیتو: (غصے سے) نان سنز (NON SENSE) ایک دم نان سنز سب گڑبڑ کر دیا۔ پھر کہو۔ سانپوں پہ سینے نہیں سینے پر سانپ اور خون میں آنکھیں نہیں۔ آنکھوں میں خون۔ پھر کہو۔

گھسیٹا رام: جی میں ذرا تھک گیا ہوں۔ تھوڑا سا شربت بنفشہ پی لوں۔ آپ شنگار بیگم سے ریہرسل کرائیے۔

دھوم کیتو: اچھا پی لو۔ (شنگار بیگم سے) ہاں شنگار بیگم۔ اپنے چہرے پر رنج و غم کے جذبات پیدا کرتے ہوئے کہئے۔ "یہ سب قسمت کی بات ہے پریم ڈارلنگ! میری قسمت میں یہی لکھا تھا کہ میں گھل گھل کر مر جاؤں۔"

شنگار بیگم: یہ سب پریم کی بات ہے قسمت ڈارلنگ۔

دھوم کیتو: پریم کی بات نہیں۔ قسمت کی بات۔
شنگار بیگم: یہ سب قسمت کی باتیں ہیں گھسیٹا رام۔
دھوم کیتو: گھسیٹا رام نہیں۔ پریم کمار۔
شنگار بیگم: یہ سب پریم کمار کی بات ہے قسمت ڈارلنگ۔
دھوم کیتو: نان سنز۔ ایک دم نان سنز۔ دیکھئے آپ کو یہ فقرے کہتے وقت مسکرانا نہیں چاہیئے۔ یہ نہایت ٹریجک سین ہے۔ پھر کہیئے۔
شنگار بیگم: یہ سب قسمت کی بات ہے پریم ڈارلنگ۔
دھوم کیتو: شاباش۔ بالکل ٹھیک۔ آگے کہیئے۔
شنگار بیگم: آگے تو میں بھول گئی۔ کہوں کیا تمہارا سر۔
دھوم کیتو: نان سنز۔ ڈائرکٹر کو اس طرح سے مخاطب کیا جاتا ہے۔ معافی مانگیے۔
شنگار بیگم: اونہہ۔ آئے بڑے ڈائرکٹر۔ نہیں مانگتی۔
دھوم کیتو: معافی مانگنی پڑے گی۔ کہیئے۔ "مجھے بہت افسوس ہے"۔
شنگار بیگم: نہیں کہتی۔ اگر آپ مجبور کریں گے۔ تو میں آپ سے روٹھ جاؤں گی اور ساری عمر نہیں بولوں گی۔
دھوم کیتو: میں کہتا ہوں۔ ضد نہ کرو شنگار بیگم۔ معافی مانگ لو۔
شنگار بیگم: جایئے۔ نہیں مانگتی۔
دھوم کیتو: اُف۔ سارا چوپٹ ہو گیا۔ بتاؤ گھسیٹا رام۔ جلدی بتاؤ۔ اب میں کیا کروں؟ بڑی ضدی عورت ہے۔

گھسیٹا رام : میں بتاؤں آپ کیا کریں۔

دھوم کیتو : ہاں ہاں کوئی تدبیر بتاؤ۔ یہ تو ایکدم روٹھ گئی۔

گھسیٹا رام : آپ اس سے معافی مانگ لیجئے۔

دھوم کیتو : میں معافی مانگ لوں . . . ہاں ہاں۔ ٹھیک ہی تو ہے۔ اچھا شنگار ، ڈارلنگ مجھے معاف کر دو۔

شنگار بیگم : (ہنس کر) اب آئے نہ سیدھی راہ پر۔ بڑا رعب جماتے تھے ، ڈائرکٹر کہیں کے۔

دھوم کیتو : شکر ہے۔ تمہارا موڈ تو ٹھیک ہوا۔ اچھا ریہرسل ختم باقی سیٹ پر کریں گے۔

ساتواں منظر

(سیٹھ دمڑی پرشاد کا کمرہ)

(سیٹھ دمڑی پرشاد کچھ فلمی رسالے اور اخبارات پڑھ رہے ہیں۔ دھوم کیتو داخل ہوتا ہے)

دھوم کیتو : آداب عرض۔ سیٹھ صاحب۔

دمڑی پرشاد : اوہ۔ ڈائرکٹر صاحب۔ آداب عرض۔ آداب عرض۔ تشریف رکھیئے۔ بھئی آپ نے تو کمال کر دیا۔ ہر فلمی رسالے میں کلا ونا شش عرف ستیاناس کا اشتہار۔ ہر اخبار میں اس کے چرچے۔

دھوم کیتو : آپ کی دعا ہے۔ سب ایڈیٹر اپنے دوست ہیں۔ اور نہ بھی

ہوں۔ تو نقد نارائن کی برکت سے بنائے جا سکتے ہیں۔ ایک دفعہ تو ایسی پبلسٹی کی ہے کہ فلم ابھی ختم نہیں ہوئی اور پانچ ڈسٹری بیوٹرز کی آفرز میری جیب میں ہیں۔

دمڑی پرشاد: پانچ ڈسٹری بیوٹرز! پھر تو کام بن گیا۔

دھوم کیتو: دیکھئے سیٹھ صاحب۔ اس وقت تک پونے پانچ لاکھ خرچ آیا ہے اور پونے بارہ لاکھ کی آفرز آچکی ہیں۔

دمڑی پرشاد: پونے بارہ مت کہئے ڈائرکٹر صاحب — یہ تو پو بارہ ہیں۔ پو بارہ۔

دھوم کیتو: سب آپ کی دعا ہے۔ یہ تار ملاحظہ فرمائیے۔ (تار دکھاتا ہے) ناردرن سرکٹ کے لئے چار لاکھ۔ ایسٹرن سرکٹ کے لئے چار لاکھ۔ ویسٹرن سرکٹ کے لئے پونے چار لاکھ۔ ٹوٹل پونے بارہ لاکھ۔

دمڑی پرشاد: (خوشی سے) باپ رے پونے بارہ لاکھ۔ یعنی پورے سات لاکھ کا منافع۔

دھوم کیتو: منہ میٹھا کرائیے سیٹھ صاحب۔ دیکھئے کتنی کامیاب پکچر بنائی ہے۔

دمڑی پرشاد: کرائیں گے ضرور کرائیں گے۔ پہلے فلم ختم تو ہو لینے دیجئے۔ اچھا آخری شاٹ کب لے رہے ہیں؟

دھوم کیتو: اس سوموار کو۔ سیٹ پر ضرور تشریف لائیے گا۔

دمڑی پرشاد: ضرور۔ ضرور۔

دھوم کیتو: اچھا اب اجازت۔ آداب عرض۔

آٹھواں منظر

(سیٹ پر ہیرو اور ہیروئن آمنے سامنے کھڑے ہیں۔ اور سیٹھ صاحب کرسی پر بیٹھے ہوئے ہیں۔ دھوم کیتو سین ڈائرکٹ کر رہا ہے)

دھوم کیتو: (گھسیٹا رام اور شنگار بیگم سے) یہ آخری شاٹ ہے۔ کافی زوردار ہونا چاہیئے۔ چہرے پر ایسے جذبات ہونے چاہئیں جیسے کہ آپ دونوں کو کھویا ہوا خزانہ مل گیا ہے اور در اصل دوگانے کے بول بھی یہی ہیں۔ ہاں شنگار بیگم ذرا گھسیٹا رام کی طرف مسکرا کر دیکھیئے۔ اور دوگانا شروع کیجئے۔

شنگار بیگم:۔

مل گیا جی۔ مجھے مل گیا جی۔ مجھے مل گیا جی

میرا کھویا ہوا دیوانہ

گھسیٹا رام:۔

مل گیا رے۔ مجھے مل گیا رے۔ مجھے مل گیا رے

میرا کھویا ہوا جی خزانہ

شنگار بیگم: آج میرے من کی کوئل کوک اٹھی رے۔

گھسیٹا رام: آج مجھے ہائے بڑی بھوک لگی رے۔

شنگار بیگم: آج میری آنکھوں میں خمار سا ہے کیوں۔
گھسیٹا رام: آج مجھے چڑھ رہا بخار سا ہے کیوں۔
شنگار بیگم۔ گھسیٹا رام: سہ
مل گیا رے۔ مجھے مل گیا رے۔ مجھے مل گیا رے
میرا کھویا ہوا جی خزانہ
دھوم کیتو: کٹ (CUT) شاٹ ختم

نواں منظر

سیٹھ دمڑی پرشاد کا دفتر

(دھوم کیتو۔ گھسیٹا رام۔ شنگار بیگم اور باقی ایکٹر جنھوں نے کلا وناش عرف ستیاناس میں کام کیا۔ سیٹھ دمڑی پرشاد کے دائیں بائیں بیٹھے ہوئے ہیں)

دمڑی پرشاد: لیڈیز اینڈ جنٹلمین! یہ چھوٹا سا جلسہ میں نے اس لئے منعقد کیا ہے کہ آپ سب لوگوں کو مبارکباد پیش کی جائے۔ آپ لوگوں کو یہ سن کر بہت خوشی ہوگی کہ "کلا وناش عرف ستیاناس" نے ہر جگہ کامیابی کے نئے ریکارڈ قائم کئے ہیں۔ بمبئی میں چالیس ہفتے۔ دہلی میں تیس ہفتے۔ آگرہ میں بیس ہفتے۔ جالندھر میں پچیس ہفتے اور ناگپور میں بتیس ہفتے۔

سب ایکٹر: (تالیاں پیٹتے ہوئے) مبارک! مبارک۔ مبارک۔

دمڑی پرشاد: میں اس مبارک موقعہ پر کچھ انعامات تقسیم کرنا چاہتا ہوں۔

سب ایکٹر: ارشاد۔ ارشاد۔ ارشاد!

دمڑی پرشاد: شنگاری بیگم کو یہ انعام دیا جاتا ہے کہ آج دوپہر کو میں اس سے شادی کروں گا۔ بشرطیکہ ڈائرکٹر صاحب کو کوئی عذر نہ ہو۔

دھوم کیتو: مجھے بالکل کوئی عذر نہیں ہے۔

دمڑی پرشاد: شکریہ۔ ڈائرکٹر صاحب کو فلم ڈائرکٹ کرنے اور شنگاری بیگم کے معاملے میں فراخدلی دکھانے کے لئے ایک سیکنڈ ہینڈ بائیسکل پیش کی جائے گی۔ اس کے ساتھ ہی میری اگلی فلم "سرو ناش عرف بکواس کو وہی ڈائرکٹ کریں گے۔

دھوم کیتو: شکریہ۔ بہت بہت شکریہ۔

دمڑی پرشاد: گھسیٹا رام کی خدمات کو سامنے رکھتے ہوئے میں نے یہ فیصلہ کیا ہے کہ انھیں ایک ریشمی بش شرٹ سلوادی جائے۔ اور باقی ایکٹروں کی خدمت میں کانپوری چپل کا ایک ایک جوڑا پیش کیا جائے گا۔

سب ایکٹر: شکریہ۔ بہت بہت شکریہ۔

دمڑی پرشاد: جلسہ ختم ہونے سے پہلے سب لوگ مل کر تین دفعہ نعرہ لگائیے۔۔۔۔ کلا ونا ش

سب ایکٹر: زندہ باد۔

دمڑی پرشاد: ستیاناس

سب ایکٹر: زندہ باد۔
دمڑی پرشاد: سیٹھ دمڑی پرشاد!
سب ایکٹر: زندہ باد۔

(پردہ)

دوست رہنما فلسفی

نام تو ان کا کچھ اور ہے لیکن محلے میں وہ چچا افلاطون کے نام سے یاد کئے جاتے ہیں اور سچ تو یہ ہے کہ ان کے سن وسال کو مدنظر رکھتے ہوئے اس سے بہتر لقب ان کے لئے تجویز نہیں کیا جا سکتا تھا۔ محلے میں ان کی حیثیت دوست رہنما اور فلسفی کی ہے۔ یعنی وہ محلے میں رہنے والے ہر شخص کے دوست ہیں چاہے وہ شخص انھیں دوست سمجھے یا نہ سمجھے۔ رہنما ہیں چاہے وہ ان پر ایمان لائے یا نہ لائے اور فلسفی ہیں چاہے ان کی باتوں میں مغز ہو یا نہ ہو۔ دراصل چچا افلاطون اس بات کی پرواہ نہیں کرتے کہ دوسرے لوگ ان کے متعلق کیا رائے قائم کرتے ہیں۔ اگر پرواکرتے تو پھر وہ چچا افلاطون نہ ہوتے۔ ہماری اور آپ کی طرح "دفتر" میں قلم گھسا کرتے یا دکان پر سودا سلف بیچا کرتے۔

چچا افلاطون کو جس وقت پتہ چلتا ہے کہ محلے میں کسی شخص پر مصیبت آنیوالی

ہے یا آئی ہے وہ فوراً اس کے پاس پہنچتے ہیں اور اس کو اپنے مشوروں سے فائدہ اٹھانے کا موقع بہم پہنچاتے ہیں۔ پچھلے دنوں میری نظر کمزور ہوگئی۔ آنکھوں کا معائنہ کرایا۔ ڈاکٹروں نے عینک استعمال کرنے کا مشورہ دیا۔ عینک بنوانے جا رہا تھا کہ راستے میں چچا افلاطون سے ملاقات ہوگئی۔ انھوں نے کہا۔

"دماغ چل گیا ہے تمھارا۔ اس عمر میں عینک لگا رہے ہو بڑھاپے میں کیا کروگے؟"

"بڑھاپے میں؟ ظاہر ہے کہ بڑھاپے میں بھی عینک استعمال کروں گا۔"

"میاں ہوش کی دوا کرو۔ اگر جوانی میں عینک لگاؤ گے تو بڑھاپے میں تو ضرور اندھے ہو جاؤ گے۔"

"تو بتائیے پھر کیا کروں؟"

"دیکھو عینک لگوانے کا خیال ترک کردو۔ آنکھوں میں صبح شام بادام روغن ڈالا کرو۔ اگر دو ہفتوں بعد دن کو تارے نظر نہ آنے لگیں تو چچا افلاطون نام نہیں۔"

"دن کو تارے نظر نہ بھی آئیں تو کوئی مضائقہ نہیں۔ رات کو نظر آجائیں تو بھی غنیمت ہے۔"

"نہیں نہیں اپنی قسم دن کو نظر آئیں گے آزمودہ نسخہ ہے۔ بس بادام روغن کے تین قطرے صبح اور تین قطرے شام۔ عینک کی ضرورت نہ رہے گی۔

دو بلکہ چار ہفتے آنکھوں میں روغن بادام ڈالتے رہے۔ نتیجہ یہ ہوا کہ رات کے وقت جب چاند کی طرف دیکھتے تو وہ تارا نظر آتا تھا۔ اور جب تاروں کی طرف دیکھتے تو مطلع بالکل صاف۔ اس کے ساتھ سر میں اس قسم کا درد کہ دھاڑیں مار کر

رونے کو جی چاہتا۔ دوبارہ آنکھیں ٹیسٹ کرائیں۔ ڈاکٹر نے بتایا کہ عینک کا نمبر پہلے کی نسبت بڑھ گیا ہے اس لئے عینک بنوانے میں مزید دیر نہیں کرنی چاہیے۔ عینک لگوائی لیکن چچا افلاطون اس دن سے ناراض ہیں کہتے ہیں یا تو تم آنکھوں میں روغن بادام ڈالتے نہیں رہے یا پھر وہ بادام روغن گھٹیا درجے کا تھا۔

ہمارے محلے میں ایک بی اے پاس بیکار نوجوان رہتے ہیں۔ چچا افلاطون کو کسی نے بتایا کہ وہ دو سال سے بیکار ہیں۔ یہ سن کر انھیں بہت افسوس ہوا اسی دن نوجوان کو گھر بلا بھیجا اور کہنے لگے۔

"تم نے مجھے پہلے کیوں نہ بتایا کہ تم اتنے عرصے سے بیکار رہو؟"

نوجوان نے عاجزی سے کہا۔ "غلطی ہوئی معاف کر دیجیے۔"

چچا افلاطون نے الماری سے ایک کتاب نکالی دو چار منٹ اس کے ورق الٹتے رہے اور پھر نوجوان سے مخاطب ہو کر فرمایا۔

"دیکھو برخوردار۔ مایوس ہونے کی ضرورت نہیں۔ بیکار لوگوں کے لئے ہزاروں کام اس کتاب میں درج ہیں۔ پہلے یہ بتاؤ کہ تم مچھلیاں پکڑنا پسند کرو گے یا مینڈک؟"

نوجوان نے حیران ہوتے ہوئے کہا۔ "میں آپ کا مطلب نہیں سمجھا۔"

"مطلب یہ کہ اگر تم ہر روز پچاس مچھلیاں یا پچاس مینڈک پکڑ سکو تو انھیں فروخت کر کے کافی روپیہ کما سکتے ہو۔ مچھلیاں تو وہ لوگ خریدیں گے جنھیں کھانے کا شوق ہے اور مینڈک تم ان کالجوں میں فروخت کر سکتے ہو جہاں علم حیوانات پڑھایا جاتا ہے؟"

"معاف کیجئے یہ کام مجھ سے نہ ہو سکے گا۔"

"خیر کوئی بات نہیں۔ اچھا نہ کرو۔ جنگلی بندر پکڑ لو گے؟"

"جنگلی بندر! یہ تو اور بھی مشکل کام ہے۔"

"اچھا اسے بھی رہنے دو۔ تمھارے لئے کوئی اور کام ڈھونڈتے ہیں۔"

چچا افلاطون نے پھر کتاب کھولی اور تھوڑے وقفے کے بعد خوشی سے چلّا کر کہا۔" مل گیا۔ مل گیا۔"

نوجوان نے کہا۔" فرمائیے۔"

"تم جنگلی شہد اکٹھا کر کے فروخت کیا کرو معقول آمدنی ہو سکتی ہے۔"

نوجوان نے ڈرتے ڈرتے کہا۔" لیکن یہ تو ذرا ٹیڑھی کھیر ہے۔"

"ذرا بھی ٹیڑھی نہیں۔" چچا افلاطون بڑے وثوق سے بولے۔" تم شاید شہد کی مکھیوں سے ڈرتے ہو۔ انھیں بھگانے کی ترکیب میں بتلائے دیتا ہوں۔ دیکھو خوب ابلتا ہوا پانی شہد کے چھتے پر ڈال دو۔ تمام مکھیاں چھتے سے گر کر ڈھیر ہو جائیں گی۔ بس اطمینان سے چھتے سے شہد نچوڑ وا اور بوتل میں بھر لو۔"

چنانچہ وہ نوجوان شہد کے چھتوں کی تلاش میں روانہ ہو گیا۔ بڑی دوڑ دھوپ کے بعد ایک جنگل میں اسے ایک بہت بڑا چھتہ نظر آیا۔ وہ درخت پر چڑھ گیا۔ لیکن اس سے پہلے کہ وہ چھتے پر گرم پانی انڈیلتا سینکڑوں مکھیوں نے مل کر اس پر حملہ کر دیا۔ گھبرا کر نوجوان درخت کے نیچے جو گرا تو ٹانگ ٹوٹ گئی۔ تین مہینے ہسپتال میں پڑا رہا۔ چچا افلاطون بھی حال پوچھنے گئے فرمانے

لگے۔" تم نے غلطی کی کہ چھتے پر گرم پانی پچکاری سے نہیں ڈالا۔ اگر پچکاری استعمال کرتے تو مکھیوں کی کیا مجال تھی کہ تمھیں کاٹتیں۔ خیر آئندہ خیال رکھنا۔

ہمارے محلے میں ایک خاندانی رئیس بھی رہتے ہیں۔ انھیں جانور پالنے کا بہت شوق ہے۔ ایک دفعہ ان کا ہرن گم ہوگیا۔ وہ بہت پریشان ہوئے کیونکہ ان کے ہاں ہرن اور ہرنی کا ایک جوڑا تھا اور ہرن کی غیر حاضری میں ہرنی کچھ اداس اداس دکھائی دیتی تھی۔ انھوں نے ہرن کی بہت تلاش کی' اخباروں میں گم شدہ ہرن کی تلاش کے عنوان سے اشتہار بھی دیا۔ ہرن ڈھونڈ کر لانے والے کے لئے انعام مقرر کیا۔ لیکن ہرن نہ ملا۔ چچا افلاطون نے جب سُنا تو وہ رئیس کے گھر پہنچے۔

"آپ کے خیال میں ہرن کے یک لخت گھر سے چلے جانے کی کیا وجہ ہوسکتی ہے؟" انھوں نے رئیس سے پوچھا۔

"کیا معلوم۔ کچھ نہیں کہہ سکتا۔"

"آپ نے اسے کبھی سخت سست تو نہیں کہا؟"

"میں اسے سخت سست کہتا! اجی حضرت! وہ تو مجھے جان سے زیادہ عزیز تھا۔"

"آپ نے کبھی اسے وہ غذا کھانے پر تو مجبور نہیں کیا جو اسے ناپسند تھی۔"

"بالکل نہیں۔"

"آپ کبھی اس کے آرام میں تو خلل انداز نہیں ہوئے؟"

"مطلقاً نہیں۔"

"آپ نے کبھی اس پر یہ ظاہر تو ہونے نہیں دیا کہ اب وہ بوڑھا ہو گیا ہے؟"

"نہیں۔"

"تو پھر کیا وجہ ہو سکتی ہے؟"

"خدا جانے ہماری سمجھ میں تو کوئی وجہ نہیں آتی۔"

"ٹھہریئے میں بتاتا ہوں۔ معلوم ہوتا ہے کہ اس کی کسی بات پر ہرنی سے رنجش ہو گئی ہے اور وہ ....."

"ہو سکتا ہے۔"

"ہوا یہی ہے۔"

"آپ کا مطلب ہے وہ ہرنی سے روٹھ کر چلا گیا؟"

"جی ہاں۔ بالکل یہی مطلب ہے۔"

"اچھا اگر مان لیا جائے کہ آپ کا خیال صحیح ہے تو پھر...؟"

"پھر ہرن کے واپس لانے کا ایک یہی طریقہ ہے.... یعنی...."

"یعنی اسے منانے کے لئے ہرنی کو بھیجا جائے۔"

"جی ہاں۔ جی ہاں۔"

"لیکن کہاں۔ ہرن کا کچھ اتا پتہ بھی تو معلوم ہو۔"

اس کی فکر نہ کیجئے۔ یہ سب ہرنی پر چھوڑ دیجئے۔ دل کو دل سے راہ ہوتی ہے۔ وہ خود تلاش کر لے گی۔"

رئیس پہلے تو بہت جھجکا یا۔ لیکن جب چچا افلاطون نے اسے بار بار یہ بات ذہن نشین کرادی کہ اس کا گم شدہ ہرن مل جائے گا تو وہ رضامند ہو گیا۔ نتیجہ یہ

ہوا کہ ہرن تو گم ہو ہی گیا تھا اب ہرنی سے بھی ہاتھ دھو بیٹھا۔ لیکن چچا افلاطون کو اب بھی یقین ہے کہ ایک دن ہرنی ہرن کو ضرور واپس لے کر آئے گی۔

دو سال کی بات ہے کہ ایک بیوہ کے اکلوتے لڑکے کو باولے کتے نے کاٹ کھایا۔ محلے والے لڑکے کو ہسپتال لے جا رہے تھے۔ ادھر کہیں سے چچا افلاطون آ نکلے۔ کہنے لگے۔ "کیوں نازک اندام بچے کو خواہ مخواہ ہسپتال لے جاتے ہو۔ وہ لوگ ٹیکے لگا لگا کر اس کا جسم چھلنی کر دیں گے۔ اسے سخت اذیت ہوگی۔"

کسی نے پوچھا تو پھر کیا کرنا چاہیے؟"

چچا افلاطون نے کہا۔ "جس جگہ کتے نے کاٹا ہے اس پر دھتورے کے پتے گرم کر کے باندھ دو۔ چار پانچ دن میں ٹھیک ہو جائے گا۔"

چنانچہ یہی کیا گیا۔ زخم بظاہر تندرست ہو گیا۔ ہر شخص نے چچا کی فہم و فراست کی تعریف کی۔ لیکن چند مہینوں کے بعد وہ لڑکا خاص قسم کے پاگل پن میں مبتلا ہو گیا۔ وہ پانی سے ڈرتا۔ کتے کی طرح آوازیں نکالتا اور لوگوں کو کاٹنے کے لئے دوڑتا۔ چچا افلاطون ان دنوں بمبئی گئے ہوئے تھے۔ کسی شخص کی سمجھ میں نہ آتا تھا کہ کیا کیا جائے۔ لڑکے کا بہترین علاج کیا گیا۔ لیکن وہ جانبر نہ ہو سکا۔ بمبئی سے واپس آنے کے بعد جب چچا افلاطون نے اس لڑکے کی وفات کی خبر سنی تو کہنے لگے۔ "صرف ایک مہینہ محلے سے غیر حاضر رہا۔ اور میری عدم موجودگی میں تم سب مل کر بھی بچا پائے نوجوان لڑکے کی جان نہ بچا سکے۔

مجھے تمہاری بے بسی پر ترس آتا ہے۔

آجکل دنیا میں جب کہ ہر جگہ نفسا نفسی کا عالم ہے جب کہ کسی شخص کو کسی دوسرے شخص سے بات چیت کرنے کی فرصت نہیں۔ چچا افلاطون کا دم غنیمت ہے۔ ہم محلے والے کبھی کبھی سوچتے ہیں کہ اگر چچا افلاطون نہ ہوتے تو مصیبت کے وقت ہماری دست گیری اور رہنمائی کون کرتا۔

منتخب مزاحیہ مضامین کا ایک اور مجموعہ

مِس چنبیلی

مصنف : کنہیا لال کپور

بین الاقوامی ایڈیشن جلد منظر عام پر آرہا ہے